LOVE THAT SASS

C.D. GORRI

LOVE THAT SASS

Dire Wolf Mates 5
by C.D. Gorri
Edited by BookNookNuts

Copyright 2023 C.D. Gorri, NJ

For my hubby,
Thank you for your constance.
Xoxo, C.D.

Before you begin sign up for my newsletter here:
SUBSCRIBE HERE

This is a work of fiction. All of the characters,
names, places, organizations, and events portrayed

BLURB

Can a fun loving bad boy Dire Wolf find redemption with a curvy human?

Weylin Scott is the original DWMC playboy. The stud muffin Wolf has always been the love 'em and leave 'em type. All his conquests know the drill. No harm, no foul, right?

But what happens when a human with a heart of gold catches the attention of the ramblin' redhead? His Alpha says she's off limits, but his Wolf can't stay away.

Will he endanger the Pack by revealing what he is too fast, too soon?

Gwendolyn Hoffer needs to come up with some quick cash to pay for her grandfather's care at a local assisted living facility. It's slim pickings on the job market, but applying at the new roadhouse seems the perfect solution.

Raised by the former deacon to be a good girl, she vowed to save herself for marriage. But how is Gwen supposed to stick to her virtuous guns when she's surrounded by such naughty temptations?

Weylin must convince the beautiful Gwendolyn she's the only woman for him.

Can she handle the reformed playboy and deal with his furry side, too?

PROLOGUE

Gwendolyn stared at her phone as she stood in the parking lot of *Serious Moonlight Roadhouse & Bar.*

The neon pink sign cut a path across the dark night skies, and she shivered despite the jacket she wore. It was September in Blue Valley, and that meant mother nature was going through her moods. It was like the seasons had menopause. But that was typical New Jersey weather.

She wished she was looking at a message from a boyfriend or reading an email with good news for a change. Unfortunately for Gwen, it was another bill she couldn't afford. But this one had the not so subtle subject line "last warning" in bold red letters.

Dang it.

She'd already been to every restaurant and bar in a five-mile radius, which was the farthest she could go in a U-drive rideshare car with her limited budget, to apply for open positions. So far, she'd struck out.

Serious Moonlight was her last chance. With Pop's medical bills piling up, and the fee for the assisted living facility he lived in almost doubling this year, Gwen needed every dollar she could earn.

"Don't worry, Pop. I won't let you down," she whispered, pulling up a selfie she'd taken of herself and the man who'd raised her.

Pop had taken her in after her parents abandoned her and did his best to raise her with the same morals and ethics that as a deacon in the church, he valued. She did her best to abide by his rules and managed fairly well, except for a wild streak in college.

Attending art school in Manhattan meant plenty of changes for the small town Jersey girl, and Gwen had lost her heart and almost lost her virginity to a fast-talking man at the restaurant where she'd gotten a job. He'd done a number on her, and after two years, she'd come back home with her tail tucked between her legs.

Pop had welcomed her, of course, with open

arms, and she finished her degree at a local school, getting her teacher's certification as well. For a couple of years, everything was fine. She avoided men, of course, but Gwen was building a life she could be proud of.

Then Pop got sick, and they had to sell the condo to keep up with the bills. His dementia had advanced to such, she had to stay home with him, losing her teaching job in the process. The time had finally arrived where she could no longer give him the care he needed, and with a broken heart, she had him placed in the best assisted care center in the area. The price was hefty, and she hocked everything they had. But the thing about money was no matter how much you had, it never seemed to be enough.

The facility had given her thirty days to come up with the latest late payment. It was money she did not have, but she would do anything to get it. Well, almost anything.

There were things a good girl like Gwen would never do. Even if she'd sunk to an all-time low. No matter. She could live on cold cereal and instant ramen if Pop needed her to.

"You can do this," she murmured, putting her crossbody bag to rights, shoving her phone inside. "It's just a job. At a bar. A biker bar."

Her eyes went wide at the row of gleaming motorcycles lined up outside the place.

Holy crap.

She'd heard from a waitress at the last place she'd filled out an application that Serious Moonlight was the best game in town if you needed to earn money fast.

The owners were a close-knit group of friends, all drop-dead gorgeous. The latter info seemed irrelevant to Gwen, but it had been given as a sort of a warning.

Apparently, prospective employees were ferreted out if their interest in the owners was too blatant. From what she had gathered, the owners, listed as the DWMC, were so gorgeous, people just threw themselves at them.

Whatever.

Sex was not one of her motivators. Gwen was just not in the market for a fling. She'd survived one horrible relationship, and that was all the experience of the opposite sex she intended to have until the day she got married.

The owners seemed to have a good reputation, far as she could tell. Apparently, they treated their staff very well. Paid well, too, not to mention the tips, which was all Gwen needed to hear. She did not care about the other stuff.

Just then, the doors open, and music poured out into the lot. Her eyes went wide as an enormous bald man covered in tattoos held a smaller, skinnier man over his shoulder and was muttering something about *crazy females* and *jealous mates.*

Mates? Maybe he was Australian.

She watched for a moment before biting the bullet and heading inside. It didn't matter. She was there for a job. That was all.

"Gimme back my strippers!" someone, *a woman,* yelled from inside. Then, an older blonde woman, followed by an older man, came rushing out of those same doors.

"Patricia! You get back here!"

Oh my. What am I walking into?

Didn't matter. Gwendolyn Hoffer needed a job, and according to the Blue Valley patch, Serious Moonlight was looking for staff. It was a match made in heaven, far as she was concerned.

CHAPTER 1

Disco music blasted from the speakers and Weylin grinned like a maniac as the bachelorette party kicked it up a notch.

There were women everywhere, in all stages of dress or undress. The air was saturated with female smells, like hair product and body lotion—nothing too strong since most were Shifters. Glitter and confetti rained down from above as balloons popped and noisemakers went off.

Hell yeah. The place was simply jam packed. Women were talking, shouting, singing, and shaking their groove things all over the place. As for Weylin, well, he was in his element.

What could he say? He simply loved women. Loved flirting, making them smile. Dating was his thing, but he kept his options open. He was a free bird, *er*, Wolf, anyway. Weylin simply loved variety, and he had a whole contact list full of possibles for every night of the week.

Fun lovin'.

That was the best description Weylin had ever heard of himself. Of course, there were those who were not all that entertained by his lifestyle choices. But whatever.

Weylin could not make everyone happy. He was a Dire Wolf Shifter, not *Nutella*.

Lord, he loved the chocolate hazelnut spread! Ate it right out of the jar with a spoon if there was nothing to spread it on. Though, he had to confess, it was even better when he had a warm, willing female who didn't mind a little creative snacking.

Hmm. I am kinda hungry.

Speaking of which, it had been a few weeks since he'd gone out with a member of the opposite sex. And by going out, what he really meant, of course, was staying in. Yep, that was just what Weylin needed.

An evening with some fine, feisty woman who appreciated his brand of humor and was down for some no strings hanky panky. Even his Wolf perked up at the mention of some smexy fun times.

Grrrr.

The big, red-furred beast was easily double the size of the average Werewolf, though smaller than his Alpha, and Thor, that monster. He could more than hold his own, though, but lucky for him and everyone else, he was more lover than fighter.

Whine.

His Wolf whimpered in his mind's eye, and that brought Weylin up short. He slammed a glass down a little harder than he meant to and shook his head. Fuck. His damn beastie was getting all mushy because of all the matings going on in the Pack lately, but that sort of thing was not for him.

He was into happy endings, not happy ever afters.

Snort. What? You think guys really mature after junior high? Ha! Not likely.

Weylin's inner musings were cut short by a loud voice demanding attention. He grinned at his Pack mate, turning towards her expectantly.

"Blow jobs for everyone!" Sheila Rand, *soon-to-be-Crowley,* shouted.

As the only Dire Wolf female in their Pack, and the Alpha's actual cousin, she was something like royalty to the males who'd grown up with her. The fact she was about to become actual royalty, marrying the one and only Lion prince of the Blue Valley Pride, was just kismet.

Damn, but she was pretty as a picture. Red hair flowing around her shoulders, eyes bright with happiness. Weylin could not be more thrilled for her if he tried. Hell, he even liked her mate. Leo was a down-to-earth kind of prince, even if he was a tad bit obsessed with his hair.

Felines and their manes. Grrr.

"Shake a tail feather, Weylin! My girls are thirsty!" she crowed, slamming her hands on top of the bar.

"I'm hurrying, girl."

"Good. Make em extra strong, and for fuck's sake, do not allow Patricia near any of the drinks," she mock-whispered.

"I heard that!" yelled the sassy older Lioness.

"No worries, Sheila. I know better than that," Weylin replied and lifted the shaker up to mix the drink.

"Like my party?" Sheila asked, looking around happily.

"I do, but can I ask a question?" Weylin inquired, considering his words carefully.

"Shoot," Sheila said.

"What is with the disco? Did we fall into a hot

tub time machine and zap back to the 70s again? Lord, it was hard enough the first time," Weylin teased.

Dire Wolves aged slowly, and though his true age was nearer to seventy, he looked all of thirty to anyone else. Sheila was younger by far, and he was honestly curious about the whole direction of this bachelorette party.

"Ha! That was my future step-mama-in-law's doing," Sheila confided with a snort.

"I see," Weylin replied, and shook his head.

The Goldens had arrived a little while ago, toting a couple of male exotic dancers wearing platform boots and bell bottoms, but not much else. Patricia, their matriarch, led them, as usual.

The older, golden-haired female was Sheila's soon to be step-mother-in-law, having mated and married Leo's dad, the King of the Blue Valley Pride, Donovan Crowley. She had a gaggle of daughters, like four if Weylin could count, but he was not promising anything, and one son named George.

The crew of outrageous Lionesses were regulars at Serious Moonlight. Three of them were mated now, one to a member of the Dire Wolf MC. Brock and Ariella had a rocky start, but the sweet Lioness made his friend happy, so he didn't see a problem with it.

"Uh oh. Patricia is fondling the strippers again!" Sheila wailed.

A ruckus ensued, but before Weylin could do anything, Thor was on it. The male was a fucking giant, even among their kind. He had the stripper over his shoulder and was hauling his skinny ass outside before King Donovan could kill the bastard.

"Dammit Thor! Bring back my stripper!" Patricia wailed.

"You sure you want to marry into that family?" Weylin asked, only half-joking.

Sheila's smile was so wide as she watched the Goldens and Crowleys tug-o-war over the Lion matriarch. She grabbed the shot he offered and downed it with a shrug.

"I am sure. Leo is all mine, buddy. The Fates picked a good one," she said and winked.

Weylin just shook his head and continued mixing alcohol. Fated mates were like unicorns in his world. Shifters believed the Fates were the only ones responsible for delivering matches made in the heavens—*literally*.

Weylin never bought into all of that, but he had

to admit. Something was happening among their Pack.

The Dire Wolves were dropping like flies, getting mated, and in some cases, married, too. And wasn't that just fucking redundant? Being mated meant more to Shifters than any human piece of paper. But what did he know about it, anyway?

He was more than happy to remain footloose and fancy free. Able to sample the wares of many a female without shackling himself to any single one.

Yep. That was the life for him.

Lonely, you mean, his Wolf grumbled, and Weylin frowned.

The fuck? No. I do not mean lonely! I mean awesome.

"Come on, dude. Where are my blowjobs?" Sheila asked impatiently, clearly, she wanted to join in the fun.

"On it," he said, and got to work double time.

Sheila started tapping her fingernails impatiently. She was giggling, sure, but that didn't mean anything. Weylin knew a hunter on the prowl when he saw one, and his Pack mate was on the hunt for a good time.

No way in hell was he standing in the way of that. He looked at her hands while he shook up the shots she'd ordered, noting the dayglo pink paint.

Weylin wondered if she did that on purpose to match their logo. The Serious Moonlight sign was the same shade of neon. Sheila's design, of course.

"There you go, a dozen blow jobs for you and your ladies," Weylin said, handing her a tray filled with the silly little cocktails served in the extra-long shot glasses and topped with a dollop of whipped cream.

"Oh, and that one is a virgin for Lucy," he added with a wink, mentioning their Alpha female, who was currently pregnant and none too happy about being excluded from the more randy shenanigans.

"Perfect. Thanks, Wey," Sheila said and snatched the tray.

The disco continued to pound through the speakers and after another hour, he was ready to strangle someone. Good thing the boys weren't around, since the exotic dancers were on stage, gyrating their man bits in scandalous glitter thongs with banana hammocks in front.

Oh, it was just a bit of fun, but Weylin would hate to see what would happen if Derrick walked in and found his pregnant mate stuffing singles in some dude's panties. Let's face it, they were panties.

"Excuse me," a timid voice said.

Tingles started up Weylin's spine at the dulcet

sounds of the stranger's voice. His heart thudded and time seemed to slow.

Not a stranger, his Dire Wolf whispered.

Weylin shook his head. He'd been facing the other direction, but that would not matter to a Shifter like him. With his supernaturally enhanced auditory senses, he would have recognized the speaker if he knew them.

Nah. His Wolf must be crazy. No way did he know that voice. And yet, even though his human side didn't recognize the shy, husky tone, his beast sure as fuck seemed to.

But how? There was just no way Weylin would have ever forgotten it. The voice was clearly female.

Sweet. Husky. Mine.

Wait. What?

Blood rushed through his veins, and thunder pounded in his ears. The whole bar went silent, and the only thing he heard was his own damned heartbeat. His Dire Wolf was clawing and snapping, snarling to break free of his human skin. Weylin grunted as he wrestled with the animal, determined to keep control.

Mine.

His Dire Wolf sat, ears perked in that metaphysical realm where the beast waited to be called. It had been a long time since he saw the animal so clearly inside his head without calling him. It was like the Wolf was in control and Weylin was frozen.

No. No fucking way.

He wiped a hand over his face, blocking out the disco blaring from the speakers as he reined in his inner animal. Shit. This was not the time nor the place for his Wolf to go apeshit over a woman.

"I said, excuse me," the female stranger spoke again, closer this time.

Danger. Danger.

He was already sweating, and shaking like a leaf as Weylin turned slowly, prepping himself for whatever might greet him. Then he saw her, and his breath whooshed right out of his lungs.

She was leaning over the bar, trying to get his attention. Her clothes were normal, nothing special. Just a black shirt and a pair of jeans, but man oh man, the body they covered.

Holy. Fuck.

Petite and curvy, with hills and valleys, soft secrets and treasures, she was true perfection, all wrapped up in cotton and denim. His heart beat double time and the air seemed to sizzle with desire. Confidence and temptation. That's what she was.

Weylin didn't understand why women chose

clothes that looked close to torture devices to him, but not this one. She was clearly dressed for comfort, and that alone made her more stylish than any of the females in skintight couture dresses at Serious Moonlight tonight.

She didn't even have on makeup. Her smooth skin looked freshly scrubbed and when he sniffed, yep, he noted she'd used plain old-fashioned Ivory soap. A coating of sheer lip gloss covered her mouth, and he thought he scented strawberries, but that could've just been her natural scent.

Yum. Yum. YUM.

He was thunderstruck, and though Weylin knew a mere moment had passed, it could have been a millennium. Damn. She was beautiful. Her heart-shaped face was mere inches from his. Like a plump, ripe apple hanging on a low branch.

Tempting. Sweet. Seductive.

Clever eyes peeked up at him through short, thick lashes and she seemed unapologetic in demanding his attention. The woman was a walking, talking dare, and he was man enough to give in, no questions asked.

"Hello? Can you hear me?" she asked, nose scrunched up as she raised the volume of her voice to compete with the relentless disco beat pouring out of the speakers.

"I hear you, baby," Weylin growled.

Unable to resist, he caught her face in his hands, stealing a kiss that was just too damn sweet for words. He had no idea who this beauty was, but she was definitely in the right place at the right time. His Wolf howled inside his mind's eye, so loudly it damn near deafened him. Only one word rang clear throughout it all—*mate*.

Mate. Mate. MATE.

CHAPTER 2

As his Dire Wolf howled with the realization that he had found his one and only true and fated mate, Weylin's entire body hummed with joy.

He'd found her. His mate. The one woman in the entire universe who belonged to him, as he belonged to her, body, heart, and soul. But getting back to the body part, he mused, tilting his head and angling for better access as he delved his tongue inside her hot little mouth.

A million and one questions begged entry to his mind, but Weylin pushed them aside, wanting only to bask in his newfound happiness. Of course, it lasted only about a second and a half, which was right up until a loud *SLAP*, followed by an annoying sting on the side of his face, broke up his rose-tinted musings.

"OUCH!" Weylin yelped in shock.

His eyes went wide as the gorgeous creature backed up from the bar, wiping her mouth with the back of her hand like he had cooties or something.

What the fuck?

"Ohmygawd! What the heck is wrong with you?"

The outraged woman spat—*actually spat*—into a napkin she grabbed from the bar, wiping her mouth like he'd poisoned her.

"Me? Why'd you go and do a thing like that? I just sucked on a peppermint," he shrieked over the music, which, of course, had stopped right at that moment.

Dozens of Shifter eyes watched him and his mate, *er*, the mystery woman have their first lovers' quarrel. At least, that was how he was choosing to see it. Even after slapping him, Weylin had to admit his desire for her was a strong—*if possible, even stronger*—than ever.

"A peppermint? What does that have to—*ugh*," she muttered, a moue of disgust on her pretty little face.

"If you don't like PDAs you just have to say so,"

he grumbled, signaling the DJ to put the music back on.

"PDAs? Public displays of affection? OMG! Didn't anyone ever teach you any manners?"

"Of course they did, but I'm not the one slapping people," he growled, confused as fuck.

"Well, of course, I slapped you! I came in here for a job not to get manhandled by some puffed up playboy bartender who thinks he's God's gift to women," the woman retorted.

Sassy. Clever. And still cute as hell.

"Never said I was a gift, but you can unwrap me anytime," he replied and winked.

Unfortunately, the woman who would be his mate was not amused. His Dire Wolf snapped at him, but Weylin was at a loss. Usually, women found him charming, handsome, and easy to be with.

She looked at him like something she had accidentally stepped in. It was playing havoc with his ego, but even worse, his animal was starting to get pissed. The Wolf wanted out, figuring he could do a better job than the man. Maybe that was the issue. He just had to get her to understand what his animal already knew. They were fated to be together.

"Weylin, what is going on here?" a very pregnant, and somewhat amused, Lucy, interrupted.

A second hush fell over the crowd of partygoers, but at least the DJ kept playing. Still, Weylin's face turned bright red under their evil grins. Sheila was watching the byplay like it was an instant replay of the last disappointing Giants game.

Go Big Blue. Or don't. Sigh.

Damn human football league had nothing on the unofficial Shifters games he and his Pack loved to attend. Still, he was a loyal fan of the NY Giants, even if they had yet to meet their potential.

Weylin hated being the object of attention, especially when so many of the females at Sheila's party were evil. Okay, fine. Maybe not evil, but since he had dated a fair number of them, he imagined they were more than happy to see him get his ass handed to him by one of their own.

"Look, love, just let me explain—"

"Hi, I'm Lucy, and you are," but Lucy's eyes went round as she gave a delicate sniff of the stranger.

She flicked her gaze to Weylin, who followed suit. *Sniff*—well fuck, that explained it. Here he'd been thinking the little morsel was a Shifter who knew about mates and instant attraction, but the hottie with the body was a normal. A human.

My mate is human. Really?

Yes. Really, his Dire Wolf supplied.

"Gwendolyn Hoffer, nice to meet you, sort of," the woman replied.

Gwendolyn, he thought, sounding it out in his head. It was a nice name. Old-fashioned and sweet. He liked it. Hoped he'd get a chance to use it. If she let him.

Gulp.

Oh fuck. He'd really messed this thing up. Weylin's face fell as he watched the stranger cross her arms over her chest as she gave Lucy the lowdown. Well, her version of it. As Weylin listened, he learned she was from town and had come in looking for a job not to get felt up by some sleazy bartender.

Shit.

Hey, wait. He didn't even feel her up! He wanted to, sure, but he didn't. Hmm. Maybe he should have led with a *how are you* and not a lip lock? But damn, who could blame him? She was spectacular.

The woman was all of five-foot three, give or take, with a curvy little figure that made the beast within him wild for the woman. Weylin just couldn't stop staring at her. She had an ass that wouldn't quit, causing his Dire Wolf to growl and other parts of him to perk up as visions of those luscious globes backed up against his naked thighs swam around in his head.

Fuck yeah.

Weylin could not wait to get lost in that body. It had been a good long while since he'd been this worked up, and so damn fast, too. He thumped a fist nonchalantly against his dick just to settle the damn thing down.

Meanwhile, his eyes ate her up from the top of her head, covered with long, dark hair down to her warm, clever brown eyes, and that figure—*good gods*. He could come just looking at the creature.

He was practically panting for her, and for all his years, that was saying something. He'd become an addict in a moment, but he was Wolf enough to admit it. If only he could go back in time and start over.

"He meant well, I am sure. You know how it is, good-looking guy gets over-confident, assumes every girl is into him," Lucy was trying to explain away his bad behavior.

He hoped she would forgive him, let him start again. Hell, he needed her to, but when Gwendolyn looked at him, it was not with the same heated glow he knew was shining in his own poignant stare.

In fact, the woman looked at Weylin like he was a

cockroach crawling across her shoe. Equal parts fear and revulsion. Shit. This was not doing any favors for his self-esteem.

Not good, dude. So not good.

He never had a woman hate him on sight. Never mind, one he was decidedly interested in. And this was more than a cursory interest. If his Wolf was right, and the animal had never been wrong, the female was his. As in *HIS*—all caps.

Mine. Mate.

"Whatever. I am sure he is used to women falling over themselves to get to him, but that's just not me," Gwendolyn said to Lucy.

"I am so sorry about that. He is housebroken, I swear," Lucy replied sympathetically, as she patted the woman on the arm.

"Look, I am sorry about the slap, but he deserved it. Maybe I made a mistake coming in."

"No!" he shouted, biting his tongue when both women jumped.

Shit.

"I'm sorry," he grumbled.

"I just came in for a job, not to get involved in whatever this is with you guys," she said, signaling between the two of them.

"What? Ohmygawd! You think we are together?

No. We are not an item," Lucy hurried to explain, and he could have kissed the Alpha fem.

"You're not?" Gwendolyn asked, eyebrows arched.

"Hell no. Um, Weylin is like my brother. My very poorly behaved brother."

"I see," Gwen replied, a tight smile on her face. She looked like she wanted to bolt.

Fuck.

"Well, Wey, what do you have to say for yourself?" Lucy hissed the question, and he could tell the Alpha fem was pissed.

"Uh," he mumbled, and glanced from the angry pregnant female Shifter to the shocked and maybe pissed off human. Rubbing the back of his head with one hand, Weylin shrugged and said the only thing he could think of.

"You're hired?"

CHAPTER 3

A *few minutes earlier...*

Gwen swallowed back her fear, trying for courage when she approached the bar where a dazzling redhead stood smiling at the group of dancing, giggling women.

Hmm.

That was odd. The entire crowd was female. Well, except for a few gyrating, almost naked men.

What the heck?

Gwen looked around. All women, almost all nude men thrusting their hips on stage, speakers blasting 70s disco—fuck. She'd crashed a party.

Oh well. She was already there. What did she have to lose?

Famous. Last. Words.

Fast forward to Gwendolyn being grabbed, kissed within an inch of her life, and almost vaulting over the bar to jump the six foot whatever hunk of redheaded hotness before her mind came back to her.

What the heck am I doing making out with some stranger?

Sure, the man could kiss, but why was he kissing her? And why was she letting him? That was it.

SLAP!

"OUCH!" the man grunted in obvious shock.

"What is wrong with you?" Gwen grabbed a napkin, wiping her drool to her utter embarrassment.

"What the heck was that for? I just sucked on a peppermint!"

She had no idea what he was talking about? But yeah, now that he mentioned it, she felt a minty coolness in her mouth after she'd swapped spit with the dude.

"Didn't anyone ever teach you any manners? I came in here for a job not to get manhandled by some puffed up playboy," Gwen hissed.

Then she was being petted and placated by a pregnant female who was also scolding the redheaded, hot boy. She was so mixed up, she could hardly follow their byplay. But two words managed to breakthrough her kiss-addled brain.

"I'm hired?" she asked, gaze going from the pregnant woman's to the man who'd kissed her stupid.

"Um, yes?" he said.

"Definitely!" the woman replied after glancing at the man.

"Whooooeeeee! YASSS!" Gwen yelled, balling up one hand and fist-bumping her other one, making a complete ass out of herself.

But what did she care? She'd just been hired! Ignoring the sexy redhead would not be a problem, she told herself, determined to keep her vow and help her Pop.

"Um, are you okay?" the woman asked.

"Yep. I am great. When do I start?"

"Um, come back tomorrow and we will begin training!"

Gwen nodded at the woman, ignoring the man as she gathered her wits and left the place. She would be back the next day where, hopefully, she would find herself with a job.

Fingers crossed.

————

What the heck am I doing back in this place? Dear Lord, if Pop could see me now—he'd probably ask for a beer.

Gwendolyn's thoughts raced from one thing to another so quickly they were liable to make her sick, but she just couldn't slow them down. At least the roadhouse was on the outskirts of town, and no one she knew would see her.

She doubted many members of the small church she belonged to, where her Pop had been a deacon, attended the raucous bar. That was one saving grace. But what did she really care? She needed money and bartending was an honest living.

"Hi Gwen! What are you doing here?" a somewhat familiar voice called out.

Dang it.

She turned her head and saw Kelly Vanderbilt running up to greet her. She'd been one of those annoyingly perky teenagers at Maccon City High School. Not one of Gwendolyn's small circle of friends, but they'd had some classes together.

"Hi Kelly. I'm training to be a bartender here," she told her, with a tight smile on her face.

Kelly was tall and blonde with a svelte physique and flawless skin. She was gorgeous in a way Gwen could never compete with, so she never tried. Why bother? She knew her limitations, and she was perfectly happy with the face and body God gave her.

"You? I thought you were like super religious?" Kelly said, though it sounded like a question to Gwen.

"Nothing against bartending in the Bible, Kelly," she teased, and the other woman laughed.

"I suppose not. Anyway, good luck. It's a good place to work, just don't break your heart on any of the guys. These boys are all dogs!" she said cheerfully and ran inside.

Gwen shook her head after the woman, tapping her fingers against her pocketbook as she followed much more slowly. She thought about what Kelly said about her being religious and supposed she had earned that rep back in school.

Oh, there were plenty of things about the church she did not agree with, but that was neither here nor there. Pop was a deacon, and she had attended services with him every Sunday. She even taught Sunday school classes when she was younger. Later, she was giving art lessons at the local preschool, but after circumstances, she'd lost that job.

She'd been so happy when Pop had been accepted into Hope Springs Senior Residence Center in Blue

Valley. It was rated the best assisted living facility in three counties, and Lord knew Pop deserved the best.

After her parents skipped out on her, Gwendolyn was left with nothing and no one. Pop was her father's father. He hadn't seen his son in years, and he didn't even know Gwen existed until a kind woman who worked for the Division of Child Protection for the state of New Jersey had tracked him down.

He'd come down to the home where the DCF agent had taken her like an avenging angel. His wife, the grandmother she was named after, had passed from cancer a few months earlier, and Pop, aka John Hoffer, had thought himself alone in the world. She could still recall the first time he came to see her…

Gwendolyn had a cut on her knee from where an older girl had shoved her on the playground and it was still oozing blood. Pop kneeled down in front of her and took a clean white hanky from his pocket and introduced himself.

"What happened there?" the old man had asked her.

"I got pushed. Who are you?" Gwen asked in return, clutching her ratty old teddy bear to her chest.

The old man had a thick mass of white streaked gray

curls on top of his head, kind brown eyes, and a smile she sort of recognized.

"I'm your grandfather. You can call me Pop, little Gwenny. Your father is my son," he explained as he cleaned my scrape.

"Dad went away with Mom," Gwen whispered, her little six year old brain trying to wrap around the enormity of what that meant.

"I see. Well, your Granny went away to Heaven a little while ago."

"Heaven? I don't think that's where Mom and Dad went. I'm sorry Granny left you," she whispered.

"Don't be. Heaven is a wonderful place where we get to see and be with all our loved ones. I will join her there someday. But not for a while."

"Oh. Maybe I could go there too."

"To Heaven? Sure you can, but not for a very long time, Gwenny. You still have stuff to do here," Pop said and smiled kindly.

It was the first time anyone had offered her such a sweet expression. Her own troubled parents were too involved with whatever had brought them down so low to pay any attention to her. She was just something extra to them.

"I'm scared. Don't wanna stay here," she confessed.

"I bet you are, but I am here now. You know, I got a

big house with plenty of room for a little girl, a yard, too. I was thinking we could keep each other from being lonely. So, what do you say?"

"Okay."

"Well, okay, then," Pop said and smiled, offering a hand.

The two of them had been inseparable since that moment. He'd been a deacon at the small church on Main Street, and Gwen had attended services with him. But all her religious studies had done nothing to curb Gwendolyn's wild side. In high school, she'd been a tad rebellious, sneaking off to the Big Apple to take in the sights and museums. Yeah, she might have danced her butt off a bit, too.

In college, she did more of the same. Majoring in art, she had hoped to work in a museum or gallery. She just loved the multi-cultural climate and the bright lights and artistic richness of city life. Then her heart got stomped on by a boyfriend and she'd run back home.

That was almost eight years ago. Gwendolyn had done her best to stay optimistic and true to her promise ever since. It was easy. She'd simply sworn off men.

"Hey, you coming in?"

Gwen looked up to see Lucy standing by the bar's

front door, hands on her belly. She wore a pair of black leggings with a tight shirt pulled over her stomach and a loose flannel she'd left open on top of that. She looked comfortable and cute as a button, Gwen thought, and secretly wished she had the nerve to wear tight clothes when she was pregnant someday.

"Yeah, I'm coming," she said, jogging, so the expecting mother did not have to wait in the fall breeze.

"I gotta say I am happy you came. I wasn't sure you would be back," Lucy said as she showed her the way to the employee breakroom.

There were a few lockers against one wall, and Lucy gestured to one Gwen could use. She thanked her and hung up her thin jean jacket and purse.

"So, where do we start?"

"Well, first we have some paperwork, but I am starving. How about lunch?"

"Lunch?"

Gwen's stomach was rumbling at the mere mention of food, and she could have died of embarrassment. Ever since Pop got sick, and she found she needed more and more time off to care for him, she'd been living paycheck to paycheck.

Food was a luxury these days, curvy body or not.

Her eating habits had become heavily dependent on what she could afford. She didn't regret spending all her cash on her grandfather's care, after all, she would not have him forever.

"Um, I'm sorry I am on a budget—"

"What? Oh, no. It's on the house. Derrick, he's my man and the big boss, anyway, he insists all the staff be acquainted with the menu, and I have a hankering for a double bacon brisket burger with brie, caramelized onions, and fig jam!"

"What?" she laughed at what was clearly a pregnant woman's fantasy burger.

"Don't knock it till you tried it," was all Lucy said as she led the way to a table by the kitchen doors.

A big man with blond hair held back by a bandana came out of the kitchen, mumbling beneath his breath. He stopped short when he saw Lucy and Gwen.

"Hey Lucy, is this the new hire? I'm Brock," the man said, introducing himself.

"Gwen," she replied, trying to keep her eyes inside her head.

The man was gorgeous. Then again, so was everyone she'd met so far. Of course, Weylin, the redhead who'd kissed her last night, was by far the most handsome. Not that it mattered, she reminded herself firmly.

"What can I get you ladies?" he asked, as Sheila, the stunning redhead whose party it was she crashed the night before, came over.

"Brie burger for me rare," Lucy said without hesitation.

"Same!" Sheila said, sliding into a chair beside her.

"Got it, and for you?" Brock asked.

"Um, I don't know—"

"Come on, Gwen. You have to try it," Lucy said encouragingly.

She imagined the tiny pregnant woman could entice the devil to drink holy water with those puppy eyes of hers and that wide smile. She was positively beguiling.

"Okay fine, I will have the brie burger also, but medium rare, please."

"As you wish," Brock replied and winked before stalking back to the kitchen.

"So, what are we doing?" Sheila asked when a third woman came running in and joined them at the table.

"Hey girls!"

"Tracey! When did you guys get back?" Lucy asked, hugging the woman up tight.

"About ten seconds ago," a tall man answered for her, his smile wide and indulgent as the woman, Tracey, hugged Sheila next.

"Hi, I'm Tracey. Who are you?"

"Um, Gwen, I'm going to be working here," she replied, smiling back at her.

How could she not? The woman exuded joy, and her grin was contagious. The man with her was clearly one of the owners of the bar, tall, muscular, and hotter than a rockstar, Gwen mused with a shake of her head.

"I'll be back. Have to check in with Derrick," Phoenix said, kissing Tracey quickly before he walked away.

"Hey Brock, put on another burger for Tracey," Lucy screamed, smiling like a maniac. "I am so glad you guys are back. I thought you were going to miss the birth!"

"Not on your life," Tracey told her.

Gwen sat, just absorbing their energy, and listening while trying to remain unobtrusive. As if sensing it, Lucy steered the conversation to include her, and she had never felt such gratitude.

They were really something. This group of beautiful females and their equally beautiful men, Gwen thought. Each of their guys checked in on them at some point during their hour long lunch, either texting or physically dropping by. It was not something she had much experience with, and Gwendolyn was intrigued.

"Okay, I have a question," she asked, tummy full of the unsurprisingly delicious burger and hand-cut fries she'd gorged herself on.

"Shoot," Lucy asked, going to town on the triple crème raspberry and white chocolate cheesecake she was eating for dessert.

"Did you guys like special order your boyfriends from a catalog or something?" she asked point blank.

The three women blinked, looked at each other, then busted out laughing. Tracey was wiping her eyes while Lucy held onto her pregnant belly and chuckled.

"Why do you ask that?" Sheila wanted to know.

"Well. I just never saw such good-looking men be so attentive and caring to their significant others. Seems too good to be true," she said with a shake of her head.

"Okay, there's a story there, woman, spill," Lucy commanded.

Well crap. Of course, that happened. Gwen

should have known better than to open that can of worms, but she was trapped now.

"Usual story. Small-town girl moves to the big city, becomes infatuated with a fast-talking handsome man, who uses her, empties her bank account, and breaks her heart."

"The rat!"

"Got a name? I can have his legs broken by midnight," Lucy growled, and Gwen laughed, stopping when she realized no one else was.

"Oh, um, no, that's okay. I was raised by my grandfather, who was a deacon at our church. He taught me you reap what you sow, and believe me that, pardon my French, asshole is going to get what he deserves," Gwen told the three women who seemed to settle a little after that.

"So, you were raised by your grandfather?" Sheila asked.

"Yep. Pop is all I have. He's older now, and I couldn't care for him anymore. I got him a place though, at the Hope Springs assisted living facility. It's truly the best place for him with his advancing dementia and osteoporosis."

"I've heard of that place. It's a fortune if you can get in," Tracey said, nodding.

"Yep. That's why I'm here. I need this job desperately, but I swear I will work my butt off. Please don't think I told you that because I am looking for sympathy. I am a hard worker and I used to tend bar in the city, so I am sure I can keep up," she blurted.

"Hey, easy girl. Look, I have really good instincts about people, and I believe you, Gwen. Besides, Weylin already said you were hired," Lucy stated, eyes sparkling with humor. "After he kissed you silly."

"He kissed her!" Tracey whisper-screamed, and Gwen felt heat rush to her cheeks.

"He did. But it was a mistake," she explained, tucking her curly locks behind her ears.

"A mistake? How is kissing you a mistake?" Sheila asked loudly, just as *he who should not be named* walked into the bar.

The girls all giggled from where they sat in the dining room section, and Gwen whished the floor would just open up and swallow her. What was she getting herself into?

He nodded a hello to the table at large, and she felt curiously sad that he didn't come over to say hi personally. But why should that be? It wasn't like Gwen wanted him to single her out or anything.

"Alright, let me get this straight. Weylin kissed you when you came in for a job during Sheila's party and now you are going to work here, but you don't want him to kiss you anymore—is that right?" Tracey asked.

"Yep. She is here to work, not make whoopee with that redheaded he-slut," Sheila quipped.

"Is he a slut?" she asked before she could close her mouth.

"Um, no. Not really. I mean, it's not like any of us are virgins, right?" Lucy asked.

Gwen's face really flamed then. Seemed like she was way out of her league with these women, and not just because of their attractive boyfriends, but because they understood men on a level she did not.

"Oh my, are you a virgin?" Sheila asked at a decibel that made Gwen cringe.

Seemed the entire bar went quiet at the impromptu announcement, and Gwendolyn steeled herself for the blowback.

"Ladies, that is no one's business but Gwendolyn's," Lucy announced, and her glare seemed to reach everyone in the place.

Thank goodness it was early and there were less than half a dozen folks. Unfortunately, many of them were staff. It wouldn't be long till the rumor mill got finished hurling that chunk of info around.

Sigh. Might as well own it, Gwenny.

"Yes, Sheila, I am still a virgin. My choice. I made a vow to stay celibate until I found the man I was going to marry. I just haven't met him yet," she replied with a shrug.

"But I thought you said you had a boyfriend—"

"I did. In college. We had several very embarrassing discussions about my promise to wait to have sex until marriage that were very painful for me. Then I found my boyfriend in bed with my then roommate solidified my belief that I did well not to partake in anything of the kind with him."

"What a jerk! I don't blame you," Sheila said.

"Yes, he was," she replied. "But I suppose I should be thankful. If he hadn't cheated, I might have wasted more time and I would not have returned home, even if it was with my tail between my legs. See, those extra years with Pop still lucid were worth the heartache."

"Wow. Good for you," Sheila said.

"Yeah. The heck with him. And I am glad you found your way here," Tracey murmured, patting her hand.

"Bottom line, I am not here for a guy. I am here cause I need money, and I need it now. Pop's insurance plan refuses to pay for Hope Springs, they want him in a state home. I went to look at the place nearest us, and I just couldn't leave him there," she whispered, eyes filling with tears.

"Oh honey, no, don't you worry. You already got the job, now we just have to get through the formalities of training and paperwork," Lucy said, nodding her head.

"But what if Derrick doesn't think I am right for the position? I haven't met him yet, and he is the big boss, right?" she asked.

Gwen had to admit, just hearing about the man made her nervous. Meeting him was not something she was looking forward to. But with the job market being absolute crap, she had little choice.

Gulp.

CHAPTER 4

"For fuck's sake, Weylin. We do not manhandle potential employees!" Derrick growled at him from across his desk.

The Alpha obviously did not know he'd spent ten minutes wrestling his Wolf when he'd walked into the bar and saw Gwendolyn with three of the Pack females surrounding her. Fuck. She looked so beautiful. Curly brown hair, big inviting eyes, totally kissable lips just sitting there so perfect, waiting for a guy like him to come and worship at her altar.

Mine.

The animal wanted to claim her right there, but his human half recognized the obstacle to his own *happily ever after* ending. His mate was a normal. She knew fuck all about his world, and there was no way for him to explain what she meant to him without outing them all.

The problem? It wasn't his decision to make. At least, not alone, it wasn't. Which led to why he was in his Alpha's office having his ass handed to him by one angry as fuck Dire Wolf.

"I didn't know she was a potential employee, Derrick. Shit, I was completely unprepared, I know, and I apologize," Weylin explained, eyeing the enormously pissed off male.

He thought better of it and dropped his gaze as his Alpha growled menacingly. The guy was super touchy ever since his uber-pregnant wife refused to give up her hobbies despite being so late in the pregnancy. Overprotective? Maybe, if she were a typical pregnant woman, but Lucy did not do things like knit booties or bake cookies.

Her hobbies included bartending till three in the morning, dancing on bar tops despite her swollen feet, and stealing her mate's motorcycle for middle of the night rides with Sheila and those crazy Golden Lionesses. All the Shifter women he knew were hardheaded and sassy as fuck. But that's what made them so damned lovable, or so he assumed.

It drove Derrick bonkers, and that alone was worth it in his not so humble opinion. His Alpha seemed to have it coming, trying to tell that Feline what to do. Hell, that was like taking his life, *make that his balls*, in his own hands. Poor Derrick. He might be the toughest Dire Wolf of them all, but his petite mate had him wrapped around her furry little pinky.

Personally, Weylin did not see what the big deal was. Lucy was a Shifter. If she wanted to ride motorcycles, dance on a pole, and shake her sass all night long, so what? She could handle herself just fine.

Easy for him to say as an unmated male. Suddenly he pictured Gwendolyn—*damn he loved her name, it was every bit as cute as she was*—taking part in the same activities Lucy preferred, and his stomach twisted in knots.

Fuuckk.

Weylin hadn't even mated her yet, and already the woman had his balls in a vise. And this was why he was not looking for a mate! But even as he had the thought, Weylin took it back. He might not have been searching for his mate, but she landed right in his lap, and dammit, he wanted her. Fuck yes, he did! He wanted the female with every fiber of his being.

"Look, I get it, Weylin. You're single, good-looking, and you haven't met your mate yet, but at your age you should know better than to just grab random normals and shove your tongue in their mouths! For fuck's sake, I am telling you, this gigolo lifestyle of yours has to end!"

"Actually Derrick, I don't think that will be a problem because, you see, I have met her. My mate. I mean, I have met my mate," he said, feeling tongue-tied.

"Your mate? Fantastic! Wait. Fuck, please tell me it's not that other loopy Lioness, right?"

Derrick's face went from happy to horrified in the span of a millisecond. Loopy Lioness? Weylin was utterly confused.

"What or who are you talking about?" Weylin asked.

"The last single Golden girl from the Blue Valley Pride. Those females whose names all start with A! It's not her, right? I don't think I can handle another one of them in the Pack," Derrick grumbled, and ran a hand over his face.

Rigghhht.

Weylin barked a laugh, clapping his hand over his mouth at the angry glare from Derrick. The man was apparently not kidding. Weylin figured it made sense, though.

The Goldens had quite the rep, but they were fine females, if a little rascally. What did anyone expect with a mother like Patty? The new Queen of the Pride was well known for her shenanigans—*most of which involved catnip, alcohol, and dancing on top of bars or swimming naked in fountains.*

King Donovan was one lucky or unlucky male, depending on how you viewed his current cup. Weylin was a half full kinda guy. With a mate like Patricia, the Lion King would never be bored. There was something to say about that, for sure!

Now, Brock, the Dire Wolf Pack Beta, was mated to Ariella Golden. Her sister Annabeth had found her mate in a Falcon Shifter name of Hank Garret. While Antonetta had recently mated a Tiger Shifter from the Maverick Pride. If Weylin's calculations were correct, Adrianna was the last sister standing. And while they were each of them fine looking felines, alas, the last Golden was not his mate.

Besides, Weylin figured Derrick was only kidding about that whole *please let it not be her* thing. Right? Well, maybe mostly kidding.

"No, man," he told his Alpha. "My mate is not a cat. It's the woman. Her. She's it."

"What are you talking about? Who is it?" Derrick barked.

"*Her,* man. The potential employee," he whispered.

His super sensitive hearing had picked up a pair of footfalls in the hallway. The scent of berries and sweetness reached his nostrils, and he knew she was almost there. The beast in him rumbled, and Weylin coughed to cover his growl.

"The human? Absofuckinglutely not, Weylin. You can't let her know what you are," Derrick attempted to whisper.

The man was too damn loud for his own good and Weylin winced. That was so not the way he wanted to tell her about him. But it was all good, he hoped.

"Shh! They are coming," Weylin said, realizing his error in shushing his Alpha when the man growled.

"The fuck, bro. No humans. Got it?" Derrick ordered.

"Sorry, Alpha," he mumbled, baring his throat a second before Lucy opened the door.

A pair of warm brown eyes met his, and Weylin's inner beast stirred. Damn, she was beautiful. That long, curly hair fell down in ripples and he was dying to get his hands on it. Wanted to test the softness of each strand. He wondered how it would look strewn across his bed, all wild and perfect, like a dark river he would willingly wade into.

Yep. It was official. Weylin was a goner. Gwendolyn cleared her throat. Her pouty lips made a small frown as she turned her head to avoid his gaze. Damn, he hoped she didn't already hate him for what he'd done before. Maybe she was just shy, though his heart sunk at the thought of the former.

"Hey there, kitten," Derrick rumbled to Lucy, interrupting Weylin's reverie.

The Alpha's icy stare was riveted to his mate's swollen form as she walked over and dropped her cheek for a kiss. Their love was palpable in the small room. Weylin was moved beyond words as they embraced, Derrick resting one big hand on her protruding abdomen, while the other cupped Lucy's neck.

For the briefest of moments, they were as one. Heads bowed, lips touching, eyes closed. Even better, there was complete and absolute joy radiating from the pair, and it brought a rumble to Weylin's own chest. He wanted what the Alpha couple had for himself.

A mate. A family. A reason.

"Gwen, this is my, um, my guy, my fiancé, actually. Um, Derrick Rand, meet Gwendolyn Hoffer."

"Who?" Derrick asked dumbly.

"Honey, this is our new bartender, Gwen. She'll be filling in for me," Lucy said.

The Alpha stilled, hope seemed to radiate from him like rays from the sun. Watching the relief spill across Derrick's face was quite the revelation for Weylin. He was happy for the couple, but again, there was that deep longing to have that sort of bond with someone for himself.

Can have. Mate.

Shhh, he silenced his Wolf. This was not the time or place for mooning over the woman. He needed to clear the air and apologize. If he could only find the words.

"You mean it, kitten?" the big, bad Alpha asked Lucy, snagging Weylin's attention once more.

"Of course, I do—oof! Derrick! You can't just carry me off—sorry, Gwen! Weylin will finish the tour and get you the forms—oooh," Lucy yelped the last bit.

She'd been hefted in the air by her mate, who was even then nuzzling her belly with his lips, as he carted her off to another, more private, location. Weylin cleared his throat and rubbed the back of his neck. That was gonna be a hard one to explain.

"Um, wow. You know, Tracey's boyfriend did the same thing, sorta, to her after lunch," she murmured. "Does that kinda thing happen a lot around here?" Gwendolyn asked, clearing her throat.

Was he mistaken, or was that a hint of longing in her voice as she watched the Alpha pair leave? If she wanted to be swept off her feet, all she had to do was ask, he mused, a Wolfish grin spreading across his face.

"I could lie and say no, but actually, yeah, it does. All the mates, *er*, couples, are like that with each other," he began.

"Mates?"

"Oh, it's just a word we use," he said, rubbing the back of his neck harder to hide his discomfort.

"Like a club word?"

"Club? Oh, you mean motorcycle club, right? Yeah. That. Sorta," he mumbled, hating even the pretense of a lie.

"Well, where is he taking her?"

"Who? Lucy and Derrick? Oh, he's taking her somewhere to, um, show her the proper, *er*, appreciation, for her choice to stop working. You see, she's nearing the end of her pregnancy, and he's been worried sick about her. Lucy has been overdoing it with the long hours and whatnot," he said, watching the play of emotions cross her pretty face.

"Wait. Proper appreciation? Do you mean? *Ohmygah!* But isn't he worried he could, *you know,* hurt her?" Gwen asked, her nose scrunched up adorably.

"Hell no," he said and chuckled. "Derrick would cut off his arm before he hurt Lucy. She means more to him than his own life."

His blood heated looking at the woman, and the clear understanding dawned on him she could mean the same thing to him. Mates were revered in Shifter culture, Dire Wolves especially since theirs was such a long lifetime.

Mine, his Wolf growled.

CHAPTER 5

F*uck. Shit. It is her.*

Gwendolyn Hoffer was his fated mate.

Well, she could be someday. It was her choice, of course, but it was too soon to broach that subject. Still, the words felt right. This was too new and Weylin wasn't quite there yet. But he would be. Hell, he could see it approaching fast.

Gwendolyn Hoffer was important to him. Really important. His entire future was in her hands. Swallowing down his fear and nervousness, he nodded towards the pile of papers on Derrick's desk and grabbed them. Weylin stood, scrounged for a pen. He handed the whole bundle to her, shivering when their fingers touched, and little shocks of lightning zipped through him.

"Um, well, here are some forms you'll need to fill out. But you can do that at home and bring them in when you start."

"When's that?" she asked and seemed anxious.

Hmm. Why did she want to start so soon? He was curious. Weylin couldn't help it, but Weylin wouldn't hound her for answers. He'd overheard her mention financial obligations to her grandfather or something like that, but he'd stopped listening as soon as she started talking about her ex-boyfriend.

His Wolf hadn't liked that bit at all. Double standard? Maybe. But he wasn't a saint, he was a Dire Wolf and a possessive one at that. Still, it wouldn't be right to steal her story by eavesdropping, so he'd gone in search of Derrick.

Of course, Weylin hoped, in time, she would confide in him. Maybe even lean on him for support. Yeah, he would like that. For her to trust him, to think of him as more than some shmuck who'd accosted her in a bar.

Shiiitt.

"Um, how about you start tomorrow, Gwendolyn?" he asked, liking the way her name rolled off his lips.

She looked around the hallway as he led her back to the bar. All traces of the bachelorette party were gone, but Sundays were still good bar days. Gwen's eyes nearly popped out of her head as Patricia Golden arrived and jumped on the stage, where bands usually set up, leading a horrific rendition of the macarena.

"Wow. I mean, it's only three o'clock in the afternoon," Gwen murmured.

"Yeah, well, some folks start early, but uh, Patricia there is like family," he tried, then gave up when the first scarf came off the older woman's neck.

"Oh, I see, well, I am not judging. It's nice to see a woman having fun," Gwen replied, surprising him.

"Yeah, uh, oh damn, excuse me one moment, I have to stop her before she takes any more clothes off," he murmured.

"Ha!"

Gwen covered her gaping mouth with her hand. Weylin wished he could watch her some more, but he had to fix this first. He shrugged apologetically and ran past her to the stage where he hoisted the older female Lioness off the thing before she could do more than shimmy out of one bra strap beneath her blouse, thank fuck. Really, it was way too early for the Lioness' shenanigans, but maybe she was still in party mode from the night before.

"Give her here!" shouted a loud male, and Weylin willingly handed the woman over to her mate.

"Yes sir," Weylin replied automatically.

King Donovan looked pissed as hell, but he nodded his thanks. Then, he tossed his errant bride over his shoulder, smacked her on the rump, and chuckled loudly as he hightailed it out of the bar, whispering something about a stripper poll and her repeating that little dance in private.

Whatever. It was just way more info than Weylin ever wanted to hear, especially about those two. Shit. Now, where did his mate go? He jumped when she appeared before him, offering a bottle of cold water in her extended hand. Weylin took it, thanking her automatically.

"Wow. I guess stuff like that really does happen all the time in this place," Gwen murmured, worrying the chain around her neck as she sipped from her own bottle.

Weylin glanced down and saw it was a gold chain with a tiny diamond cross she held between her fingers. Pretty. He wondered where she got it. Damn, he was on fire with wanting to know more about her.

"You're staring."

"Sorry. Um, I like your necklace. That a cross?"

"Um, yeah. I got it for my Confirmation."

"So, you're religious."

"Well, my Pop is a deacon for St. Anne's on Main Street, well, he was before he got sick. Anyway, he raised me with his beliefs, I guess."

"That's interesting, Gwendolyn. I'm sorry about him being sick though," he said, truly concerned.

"He's getting on in years, and I sorta expected it. But I was raised to be a good girl, you know, boring," she said with a self-deprecating laugh.

"I don't think you're boring, Gwen."

"You don't know me," she replied, shaking her head.

"That's true. But I want to," he returned.

Gwendolyn bit her lip, then gave him a small, tight smile, before feigning interest in the papers he'd given her. That was alright. She needed time. He sensed her withdrawal and nodded his understanding. Last thing he wanted was to make her feel trapped or bamboozled by him.

"So, I should fill these out, then bring them back tomorrow, you said?"

"Yep. Come in around three and we'll start your training," he said, walking her to the door.

He noticed her checking her phone and pulling up a ride share app, and the beast in him went nuts.

Shiiitt.

"Um, I will walk you to your car. Where'd you park?"

"Oh, um, I don't drive. I was just gonna grab a U-drive," she said, naming the most popular ride share app in town.

"Um, actually, Sheila here was about to leave. I am sure she can give you a ride, right Sheila?" he called out, knowing full well his Pack mate had been eavesdropping no less than ten feet behind him.

The only other redheaded Wolf in their Pack came jogging over, a big smile on her face. Beside her was Leo, her mate and soon to be husband.

"Gwendolyn, this is Sheila and Leo, her fiancé. He's a cop," he told her, and she visibly relaxed in the big man's presence.

"Very nice to meet you, Gwendolyn," Leo said, all teeth and smiles, and Weylin had the sudden urge to punch him right in those too-pearly whites.

"Oh, I don't want to put the two of you out," Gwen said in a rush.

Too late. Sheila had already commandeered her arm and was gabbing a mile a minute about errands she had to run and how tuckered out she was and other girl shit, like where Gwen got her hair done.

Good Pack, that Sheila. She must have read his

concern through their Pack bonds and would make sure the fragile human got home safe. Gwen looked as if she would argue, feisty little thing, then she got caught up in whatever Sheila was talking about.

It amazed Weylin how quickly females could become friends, but it also warmed him to know Gwen was getting home safe tonight. The knowledge settled his beast. She paused in her tracks and her brown eyes found him instantly.

"Oh, thanks Weylin. I'll see you tomorrow," she called out and gave him a shy little wave.

"Have a good one, Gwendolyn." Weylin replied, his gaze never leaving her back for one second.

When the door finally closed, Weylin took off like a rocket, ripping the shirt from his body as he hauled ass outside a moment before his Wolf came ripping out of him.

The dark-red-furred beast was a hulking mass of muscle and angst. He followed the sound of the engine of Leo's custom '65 Stingray.

The Corvette was a work of fucking art, and being a Shifter, the Lion had it customized. A bench seat had been added in the back for when unexpected guests happened upon him, along with a titanium reinforced frame, extra absorbent shocks, and a suped up engine to name a few.

A part of Weylin was grateful the fragile human female was tucked up in the back of the big man's car with Sheila there to protect her from, well, whatever. Another part of him was barely hanging on to reason. That part was all animal. The beast didn't want Gwen in Leo's car, regardless of the fact the male was already mated.

Weylin was a Wolf. He wasn't perfect. While he accepted his imperfections as run-of-the-mill type stuff, he sure as shit didn't know he had feelings like this lurking inside him. Turned out he could be quite the possessive asshole.

Mine. Mine. MINE.

The Wolf growled and scratched. He wanted out. And he wanted out now.

She's in good hands, Wolf. Fucking relax.

But knowing all that didn't stop his animal from demanding he follow them. Weylin grunted and swayed on his feet the further she got from him. He couldn't stop himself if he tried, and why bother? He could use a run, anyway,

His transformation was fast, real fast, and his big, dark beast followed the vehicle closely as he could from the shadows of the forest beside the road. His fur was much darker than the flame colored hair that topped his head when he wore his human skin, but the hint of red was still there.

He had to be extra careful when hunting at night so humans didn't see him. Damn red fur tended to reflect in the light. Lucky for him, they tended to write him off as a large fox or stray dog. Humans didn't understand the paranormal world, and they usually ignored the things they could not comprehend.

He only hoped he didn't frighten Gwendolyn if she happened to catch a glimpse of him. Monster that he was, he'd likely scare the crap out of her. His Wolf didn't like that idea. Not one bit. But Weylin knew better than to go into this thing blind.

She was a normal. A human. And from what she'd told him, she'd been raised to be religious, moral, ethical. Shit. What the fuck did a rounder like him have to offer a woman like her?

Sweet, innocent, good girl. She deserves better.

But even those dark, disturbing thoughts did not stop his paws from moving. Oh no. He tracked her using all his skill, watched from the shadows as she got out of the car before Leo could help her—*good.*

His Werewolf senses were heightened, and he listened as she refused to go indoors until she saw them pull away. Leo had balked, but Gwen was adamant but polite. She insisted Leo and Sheila leave first and even watched them drive away.

Strange, he mused. Watching and waiting to see which house on the small residential block was hers. Only, where he would have expected her to choose a walkway, she didn't.

Gwendolyn wrapped her arms around her waist and hurried fast as her two tiny feet would take her curvy little body down the street. Weylin growled softly. Something was wrong.

He followed her for three more blocks, almost lost his shit as she turned down a road to the seedier side of Blue Valley. Right off the highway, there was a gas station, a twenty-four-hour roach coach, and a cheap motel.

His heart thudded as he watched her walk through the parking lot of the cheap motel, ignoring the catcalls from a group of guys leaning against a beat up Toyota and drinking beers from bottles wrapped in paper bags. Hell, it wasn't even dark yet.

Oh, fuck no.

Weylin snarled. The sound had been loud enough to bring a couple of heads swiveling in his direction. The distraction had allowed Gwendolyn to haul her cute little butt straight for the last room on the left side of the lot.

Shit.

If sweet little Gwen was staying here, her situation was far more dire than she'd let on. Weylin bristled beneath his fur. He wanted to bust open the door, pick her up and throw her over his shoulder, take her to his den. But he had no right to her, and he knew it.

Didn't mean he liked it, but he was not about to violate her space. Instead, he walked to the small patch of cement outside the beat up maroon painted door. Cheap black stickers with the numbers 394 were stuck on top of the paint.

He sniffed, revulsion filling him as he recognized urine from both humans and animals, chemicals, rotting food, and other revolting odors surrounding the place. The least of which was not death.

Fuck.

Gwen didn't belong there, but Weylin could not do a thing about it. Not yet, anyway. He paced back and forth, listening to the sounds of her going about what he assumed was her nightly routine.

The sun had just set, and the creeps in the lot were still lurking. It was the usual suspects, winos, and users, maybe one dealer. All human as far as he could tell, and the fact she was there was like a beacon to the evil inclined.

Weylin hated thinking of her in such a place. The lights were off, and the din of the television was low enough to suggest she slept with it on. In a place like this, he didn't blame her.

Admiration filled him as he imagined her struggle. She was smart, educated, beautiful, and she did not have the air of someone who'd grown up in a situation like this. So, this was new, he surmised.

His respect for her grew. Here he thought the woman had grit just walking into the bar to get a job. But it was more than that. Looked to him like she had given up a lot to pay for her grandfather's care. Her staying in the cheap motel, taking rideshares, and wearing simple clothing were all because she was likely putting everything she had into caring for the old man.

He didn't think people did things like that anymore. Gwendolyn Hoffer was just full of secrets and surprises, and Weylin wanted to learn them all. In due time, he told himself. For now, he would simply watch over her. Make sure she was safe.

Brave, tough girl. You can sleep tight, now. I got you.

CHAPTER 6

"No pets on the premises," the manager of the *Merry Time Motel* barked at Gwendolyn as she emerged from her room at nine o'clock the next morning.

Mr. Jacobs was about sixty years old, if she had to guess, and he had on the same dirty coverall he seemed to wear every single day as he slithered past her. He was dragging two large trash bags towards the dumpster in the back, or so she assumed, and though Gwen had heard him, she had no idea what he was talking about.

"Pets?" she asked dumbly.

"Yeah. No pets. That monster dog you got has to go. Got three complaints this morning, folks scared walking by here last night," he grunted, not bothering to look at her.

"Monster dog? And why were people walking here if this is the last unit and you are the only one who has the key to the dumpster gate?" she called back, not at all surprised he ignored her.

She tucked her still damp curls behind her ears. Crap. She was gonna be late. Gwen had no time for the strange man's delusions. Pop was getting the results back on his latest round of tests, and she needed to be there with him. She grabbed her phone, checking the app to see how long before her car would arrive.

Another two minutes. Ooh. Maybe she would have time to run to the vending machine. Gwen had forgotten to run to the all night dollar store on 3rd Street last night. They had all sorts of snack bars and things real cheap, which was basically all she could afford, and she'd eaten her last granola bar last night.

Thank goodness for Lucy's kindness yesterday. That burger had been the best thing she'd eaten all month. Who knew brie and fig jam were amazing when paired with applewood smoked bacon, and two grilled ground brisket patties with caramelized onions on top? Yep, that Brock was a certified genius in the kitchen.

Living with little to no budget meant she'd been surviving on twenty-five cent packages of instant ramen noodles and granola bars from that same dollar store for the last two months. A girl could live on less, she supposed.

Ever since, she had gotten Pop into the assisted care facility. She'd gotten kicked out of the apartment they had leased and sold off every single thing they had worth anything to pay for his treatment, care, and residence. Pop didn't have very long. Another six months or so, the doctors had said, and Gwen was determined to work her fingers to the bone to ensure he had the best care for every single minute of those six months.

Her heart squeezed in her chest as she pictured life without her Pop, and a tear came tumbling down her cheek. Stupid tears. She hated crybabies, but this was hard, and she was left all alone to deal with it.

Gwendolyn loved her Pop more than anyone on earth and she was so sad to think of him being gone, let alone to have to face the big bad world alone without him in it. The wind rustled the yellow and red leaves on the scraggly looking trees behind the motel and Gwen pulled the old cardigan she had on tighter around her body.

She wore black jeans and sneakers, and a plain

charcoal t-shirt with Pop's soft gray sweater on top. Fall was unpredictable in Blue Valley, but that was typical of all New Jersey. Hot one day, frigid the next. Today promised to be temperate with a high of sixty-nine degrees.

She snorted at that and rolled her eyes at her lameness. Somewhere inside of Gwendolyn lived a 12-year-old boy, she was sure of it. Her sense of humor certainly supported the theory.

The blast of a horn had her looking up to see a red SUV with the license plate DWM394W. Yep. It was her ride. She clicked the little checkmark on the U-drive app that told whoever needed to know she'd been picked up, and Gwendolyn walked to the passenger seat.

"Morning, Gwendolyn," a familiar voice said as a big hand beat her to the door handle.

Gwendolyn startled, a hand on her chest as she turned to find bright, familiar green eyes locked on hers. It was him. Weylin. The sexy hot bartender from last night. What was he doing here?

"Sorry. Didn't mean to scare you," he murmured, opening the door.

"No, it's my fault. Um, I'm just naturally jumpy. What are you doing here?" she blurted, hating to sound ungrateful.

"Picking you up. You ordered a car from U-drive, right?"

"Um, yeah."

"Then that's why I am here. I drive for them sometimes," he said.

But that was odd, right? Didn't he co-own Serious Moonlight? She was almost certain Kelly had mentioned all the sexy members of the DWMC all had a piece of the pie.

"Oh, I see. Sorry, I just thought you were part owner in the bar—"

"I am that, too, but anyway, *er,* what are you doing here?" he asked as he seated himself in the driver's side, waiting until she buckled her seat belt before pulling out into traffic.

Gwen didn't want anyone to know her living situation. Shame and pride warred within her, but maybe she could play it off like she'd spent the night there with someone.

Like who? A man! Sure. She could just tell Hottie McHotterson that she'd shacked up with some rando on her way home. As if doing that was better than admitting to being poor, somehow.

Yeah. Right. Soooo believable. Ugh.

She looked down at herself and snorted. So sexy. Ugh. Gwendolyn was hardly a femme fatale and certainly not a girl who rented motel rooms with strange men. She mulled it over for a minute before settling on the truth.

"I'm, well, actually, I am staying here for a while just until I can afford someplace else," she said, pride stinging her eyes.

She waited for him to judge her or criticize, but he didn't. Weylin just nodded and drove, his glittering emerald eyes on the road. My oh my, but he was handsome.

"So why are you here, Weylin, um, what was your last name?" she asked, uncertain if he'd introduced himself last night.

"Scott, it's Weylin Scott. And you are Gwendolyn?"

"Hoffer. Gwen to my friends."

"I like that. Can I call you Gwen?" he asked, a small smile tugging at the corner of his lips.

She mulled it over, getting the distinct impression he was asking for something else. Without any red flags or warning bells ringing in her head, Gwen nodded.

"You can. After all, I think it's only fair since we'll be working together."

"Good. Friends then, huh?" he asked, and pursed his lips.

Lord, help me, she thought and hid the sudden urge to fan herself.

He had the most kissable lips she had ever seen, and the fact he had actually kissed her was something she could not wrap her head around. Gwen didn't exactly garner that kind of attention from men.

Well, that was not entirely true. She had her share of admirers, but they usually gave up once they heard her hangups about sex. As in, she wasn't putting out for just anyone.

Where was she again? Oh yeah. Weylin's lips. They were a reddish pink against his pale skin, plump and softer than they appeared. After all, she had firsthand knowledge, she thought with a blush. Surprising they were so soft, she mused. Not that she went around collecting info on boys' lips or anything. But there was just something about him she found positively intriguing.

"You have the right address?" she asked.

Weylin nodded and tapped the screen on the console of the SUV to show the GPS. He had Hope Springs typed in and they were about thirty-minutes out.

"So, who's at Hope Springs? Your Pop, right? He okay?" he asked, then blanched when she stiffened.

"I'm sorry. I should not have asked you that. It's none of my business."

"No, it's okay. It's just new, you know? Yes, Pop is here, and they are making him comfortable. It's about all they can do now. He has dementia, and it seems to be advancing. With his osteoporosis, the chances of him falling and getting hurt were too great to keep him home, though I tried for a long time to manage that way."

"Is there no other family to help?" he asked softly.

"Just me. My parents left when I was about six, and I didn't even know I had a grandfather. He came down to social services the second he heard about me. Bundled me up, carted me home, and took care of me."

"Gwen, you don't have to talk about this if you don't want to," he replied, giving her an out.

"I don't mind. I mean, this is my reality."

"I appreciate that, but it's okay to need a break from reality now and then, you know? I'm sure he would want you to take care of yourself, too. From what you've said, he sounds like a good man."

"Yeah, he is the best."

Weylin reached over and patted her leg, the brief, platonic contact left tendrils of awareness racing through her, and her breath caught. Of course, her stomach chose that exact moment to go off like a bullhorn, growling loudly in the cab of the SUV. She bit her lip to hide her embarrassment.

"You hungry? I got snacks," Weylin informed her.

He leaned over to open the glove compartment where a small basket filled with trail mix, protein bars, and little bags of cheese crackers sat.

"Help yourself. There's a water right here, too," he murmured and nudged the armrest where an unopened bottle sat.

"Sorry. I didn't have time for breakfast," she said.

It wasn't exactly a lie. The whole truth was, she ran out of snacks. But this looked good. Oh well. A girl had to eat. Gwendolyn grabbed the trail mix and opened it.

Ooh, this was good stuff, she mused, eyeing the slivers of almonds, peanuts, craisins, and the little dark chocolate chunks with delight. She ate some and offered the bag to Weylin, who smiled and said thanks before snagging a handful.

He chewed with his mouth closed, which was a huge plus in her book, made small talk, and sang along with the radio. He had a nice, pleasant voice, and he knew the words to her favorite Bon Jovi songs, a must if you lived in New Jersey, and Gwen was a Jersey girl through and through.

The minutes sped by, and she found herself relaxing in his company. It was easy with him, for some reason. The interior of the SUV smelled like something woodsy and masculine, his cologne perhaps. She'd never smelled anything like it before. Pop had liked Old Spice, and she was allergic to most other scents. But not this one. This one was just fine, she mused and breathed in another gulp.

"Something wrong?" he asked, sniffing the air after her.

Shoot. She'd been caught. Gwen's face really started to burn just then, and she bit her lip. How embarrassing!

"Um, no. Sorry, it's just I have allergies to most air fresheners and perfumes, but it smells good in here and it's not bothering my sinuses. I was just trying to identify the brand."

"Oh," he said, sounding surprised.

"Um, what is it? The fragrance, I mean," she murmured, wishing a hole would open up and swallow her.

"I dunno. I don't like strong scents, so I stay away from them myself. Could be my deodorant, I guess."

Weylin lifted his arm and Gwendolyn barked out a laugh, was he smelling his own armpit? Sure enough, he did. Even offered her a go, but she just laughed it off and shook her head. It wasn't too long before he joined her in a deep, throaty chuckle.

"Guess that's silly of me," he said, and seemed embarrassed.

For some reason, that made her like him even more. Maybe there was more to Weylin Scott than met the eye. She hadn't known many men, but Gwendolyn liked to think she had a good intuition.

Danger. Danger.

The man is dangerous, Gwenny. He's a bartender and likely has a million phone numbers saved in his contact list.

She felt a stab of jealousy at the thought, but she shook it off. Gwen had no reason or right to be jealous of the man. They weren't dating or anything. She had no time for that nonsense at all. With all her hangups, it would take a man with the patience of a saint to break through her barriers—figuratively and literally.

Weylin Scott didn't strike her as a saint. Too bad really. She wouldn't mind getting to know him better. Not at all.

Why would he need to be a saint, Gwen, when a man is all anyone could ever want?

"What are you thinking about so quiet over there?" he probed.

"Oh, nothing. My mind just wanders," she said, offering him more trail mix. "You know, I never shared snacks in a U-drive with a boy before," she blurted, and her cheeks heated with embarrassment.

Weylin's grin got bigger, and he held out his hand for more of the stuff. Gwen obliged, wondering why she told him that little tidbit. She watched him pour the handful of salty sweet goodies into his mouth without spilling a thing.

He chewed and swallowed, winking at her when he caught her staring. She was making an idiot of herself, but she couldn't seem to stop. He was intriguing, and Gwendolyn was curious by nature.

"So, the bar must not be doing well if you're moonlighting with U-drive, huh?" she asked, worried now that she thought about it.

"What? No! The bar is doing great. I just do this sometimes when I am feeling bored," he said, smiling tightly.

"Oh, okay."

Hmm. Was he lying? He had no reason to, but she had a feeling he was holding something back from her. Odd. Very odd.

"We're here," Weylin announced, pulling into a parking spot.

"Okay, well, thank you very much," she began,

but he was already out of the truck and opening her door.

"You are fast," she murmured.

That brought another pink blush to his cheeks, and she watched mesmerized as Weylin lifted his arm and rubbed the back of his neck. His biceps looked likely to shred the t-shirt he wore, they were so dang big. Holy cow. He must work out like a madman to be so fit.

Looking down at herself, Gwen could only shake her head. No one would ever accuse her of being a gym rat. But she was who she was, and she liked her body just fine. She just wasn't made to be one of those slender females. Gwendolyn had curves on her curves, even with the lousy diet she'd been on, but you could blame the FDA for that.

The United States of America allowed way too much garbage in their food, and that alone accounted for the increase in obesity and disease among the poorest of its citizens. Other countries did not have that problem, something Gwen had become aware of after she'd gone to England with her high school with her honors history class.

Whatever.

She and Weylin were not an item. It didn't matter if she was chubby and poor, and he was a veritable demigod. Not that she cared about money or looks. What the heck was going on with her? She had more important things to attend to than worry over a nonexistent relationship with her new coworker.

Wake up, Gwenny.

"We going in?" Weylin asked, waiting for her to speak.

"Well, I am. I mean, I'm sure you have another person to pick up or—"

"Nope. I logged out. Figured you could use a ride back anyway, and besides, who else is gonna feed me trail mix on the way back?" he asked playfully.

Gwendolyn bit her lip and nodded. He was kind, sweet, and really freaking hot. But why was he so interested in her? She frowned.

"Look Weylin, I appreciate the ride and the fact you turned off the tipping option, but if you are here with any ulterior motives, you should know a few things about me from the start. I am not in the market for a one-night stand. I do not put out. I am not interested in playing games or being a notch on your bedpost. My Pop raised me to have a strong moral compass. I promised myself when I was sixteen that I was going to save my virginity for marriage, and I meant it."

She waited, but Weylin stood stock still, no

expression on his movie star handsome face. Gwendolyn sucked in a breath before she continued.

"I am not playing hard to get or throwing down a gauntlet. Understand? I truly believe intimacy is meant to be intimate and I am not judging anyone else for their lifestyle, but this is my body, and it is my choice to be celibate until I find *my him.*"

"Your him?"

"Yes. *My him.* My person. Someone I love, who loves me, who respects me and doesn't want to change me or ridicule me. So, if you are hanging out here cause you wanna bang the new girl, you are better off leaving. Got it?"

Weylin's green gaze seemed to glow in the crisp autumn morning, and Gwen sucked in a sharp breath. He took a step toward her, then another, and another, until Gwendolyn was backed up against the SUV.

"I can't say I've lived a celibate life, because frankly, I've been living the opposite. But I don't play with people or hearts, and I never ever stepped over the line unless someone asked me to. You don't know me yet, and you don't trust me, and that is fine. You'll learn I mean what I say. And I do respect you, Gwendolyn Hoffer. I'm just asking you to be open-minded about me. Can you do that?"

"Can I do what?" she asked, trying hard to catch her breath, but it was a little difficult with him being so close to her.

"Just don't rush to any conclusions about me you aren't sure of yet. Neither of us can tell the future, Gwen. But I can tell you this, and it is the truth, I wanna get to know you. We can go slow or fast as you like."

"Weylin—"

"Gwendolyn, I just wanna spend some time with you. Just some time, okay?"

"Why? I just told you it's not going to end in the bedroom like your other conquests. There's no point in pursuing me," she stated bluntly.

It took a sledgehammer to knock down walls. But Gwendolyn imagined she'd need a battering ram to fell this particular rampart. Of course, Weylin smiled just then, and her heart thudded even louder.

He was just too handsome. Red hair in a thousand different shades from the deepest auburn to the lightest golden flames danced in the morning breeze. Copper-colored eyelashes, so long they were positively sinful, brushed his skin with every blink of his hypnotic green eyes. Then there were his muscles —*so many muscles*—all fighting against the ridiculously tight cotton t-shirt he wore.

Whoa. Down girl!

Butterflies turned into fighter jets inside her stomach. She just could not catch her breath. The man was hot. Smokin' hot. Much too much for a chubby little homebody, goody-goody like Gwenny.

"Oh, baby, you are so worth it."

"Weylin, I mean it. I won't sleep with you," she said, but she didn't sound so certain.

"I won't push you into anything you don't want, Gwendolyn. I promise and I am a man of my word," he said, looking more serious than she had ever seen him.

"Ha! You'll get bored in a week," she snarked.

It was only the truth. Guys had come on to her before, thinking she was playing hard to get with them. But with Weylin, Gwen felt conflicted. Sad even.

What the heck?

Why should the truth make her feel so miserable? Yes, she'd made her vow very young, after a terrible teen romance that had ended the only way it could have—utter heartbreak. But Gwendolyn had never questioned or regretted her decision to abstain from smexy times.

Until now, her inner voice whispered. Gwen gasped, gaze flicking to Weylin's own questioning stare, and she shook her head. She tucked a lock of hair behind her ear, pretending not to notice the charged atmosphere between them. The wind whistled through the trees, the fall sun was still shining, but Gwen couldn't tell which way was up or down or sideways.

"Think what you like, baby. I'm not going anywhere either."

Just like that, her anxiety abided. She frowned hard, angry at herself that he should affect her so. It just wasn't her way. Despite his handsome face and pleasant demeanor, the fact remained Weylin Scott was a scoundrel. Relying on a man for her own inner peace was a foreign concept to Gwendolyn. That he should settle her upset with some words was decidedly uncool.

Heck no. That was not gonna fly.

"Well, it's your time to waste," she mumbled, giving him her back as she hoofed it through the parking lot.

His woodsy fragrance was like a drug, she thought as he caught up to her easily. Damn the man for reading her so well. It was like he knew he was getting beneath her skin.

Gwen had to actively stop herself from taking that one tiny step that would close the space between them. Her heart pounded, and her body heated. She never felt anything like it. Like she was dying for him to kiss her, but somewhere in her mind, she knew better than that.

Warning bells sounded inside her head. This man was dangerous on several levels. For one thing, he was the first guy to make her regret her promise in, well, ever. For another, just being near him made her think of all those dirty little things that happened in those naughty little romance books she liked to read in private. Only, in her version, she and Weylin were the main characters.

Sizzle.

"Are you okay?" he asked, and she realized she had stopped walking.

"What? Of course," she retorted and continued on her path.

Weylin Scott was too sexy for his own good, never mind hers. She closed her eyes and held her breath, seeming to sense the minute he backed off.

"Come on. Let's get you to Pop's appointment."

Gwen nodded and allowed him to lead her inside. She was not sure what had just happened. But it was big. Really big.

Weylin spent the morning with her at the center. He listened when she needed him to, stayed with her after the doctor left, held her when her emotions got the best of her, and even joined her when she read passages from the Bible out loud to Pop.

If she didn't know any better, she would think Weylin Scott was trying to make her fall for him. But that couldn't be. He was drop dead gorgeous, and she was, *well*, her. Men who looked like him wanted a sure thing, and she just was not that. She had told him so in no uncertain terms.

Looking at his profile now, Gwen suddenly wished she was different. Her heart squeezed. She swallowed back her regret and tried to focus on the hurt that was inevitable. They were just too different, and she was not in the market for any heartache. Gwen was not sophisticated enough for a man like Weylin.

He'll get bored and move on. Just wait it out.

Sound advice, but for some reason, it did not make her feel any better.

CHAPTER 7

I*'m losing my mind.*

The woman was driving me bananas. Or maybe it was just being close to her and not being able to do a thing about it.

Days had passed and Weylin was no closer to Gwen than he'd been since their first meeting. Okay. Not true. He actually got closer back then. At least she'd let him kiss her. Sort of. Fine, he stole that kiss.

Grrr.

His dick thumped in his jeans, and he growled in frustration. He watched her move and bit back his moan. The woman had the most glorious ass Weylin had ever seen. And he meant that in a totally non-creepy stalkerish kinda way. He just could not stop stealing glances at the thing. She was on a whole other level of fuckable.

Shit.

His jeans were too damn tight. He'd even gone commando, but that provided no relief at all. Another bite of his lip and a stifled growl as she bent down to retrieve a new bottle of simple syrup from the bottom shelf behind the bar.

Wanna bend her over. Snuggle in behind. Grab those thick thighs with my hands. Spread em wide. Fill her so deep. Yes. Yes. NO!

He should not be thinking things like that about his future mate. Well, his *would be future mate if he could only get her to pay attention to him* might be a more apt title. Problem was, the little human didn't even seem to notice.

"Weylin, I mean it. I won't sleep with you,"

Her words replayed in his head, but what could he do about it? She was not kidding when she talked about her promise to stay a virgin until she married. In his relationships before, when words failed him, Weylin had been a fan of using kisses to make up for it. Well, more than kisses, but if Gwen said no to sex, then what was a guy to do?

Not to mention the fact that Derrick had all but ordered him to stay away from her. He was to give no hint or suggestion that she was his mate. Fucking Alphahole had pretty much decided to cockblock Weylin for life!

He thought having a human mate might fuck things up for the Pack, and he wasn't having that with his own mate being ready to drop her pup any day now.

It wasn't fair. But again, what could he do about it? Weylin just wanted the same opportunity to have his own happily ever after ending that Derrick and several of the other Dire Wolves in their former MC had found. Was that so wrong?

"One part vodka, then add fresh lemon juice," she murmured, probably thinking she was speaking too low for him to hear.

If he was human, that might have been true. But he wasn't.

And therein lies the rub, he mused, with an expression of distaste on his face.

Still, it was cute the way she recited each recipe as she worked, even if she presumed it was to herself. Gwendolyn was going over a list of signature cocktails featured at Serious Moonlight that Sheila had given her when Weylin walked into the bar.

Technically, he was not supposed to work today,

but he'd asked Derrick to switch his schedule, so he had every shift she had. It was the least his Alpha could do. Lucy had supported his request, for which she had his eternal gratitude. The Alpha fem was a hopeless romantic, and she'd argued that Gwen could hardly fall for Weylin on her own without being near him.

Smart lady.

Three days had passed, and so far, nothing. That meant Weylin had seventy-two hours of staying within her periphery. It damn near killed him being so close, and yet so far. Sure, Derrick took pity on him, giving him the same schedule just to get him out of his hair.

But that wasn't enough to get the sexy as all get female to look his way. Weylin stifled a yawn. He was running himself ragged following her home and standing guard outside her door in his Wolf form every night.

What else could he do? That place was a hellhole frequented by all types of unsavory folks. Humans were bad enough, but he scented one or two supes in the area, and that did not sit well with him at all. He wished he could just take her home with him to the Pack House, but that was a no-no.

Even if Derrick allowed it, Gwen wasn't

anywhere near ready for him to reveal the truth about himself, let alone what she was to him.

"You got this," Sheila said.

Gwendolyn nodded and lifted the cocktail shaker, mobbing it back and forth at ear level. She was in the process of prepping one of every cocktail. Something all new bartenders had to do before they could pass muster.

He was pleasantly surprised watching her work. She had real potential. There was music pumping through the speakers, country western tonight, and there was already a pretty nice early dinner crowd. Some dudes were seated at the bar drinking beers, and a group of older women were having martinis and sharing a tapas tower. But none of it seemed to mess with Gwen's concentration.

Weylin had been keeping a close eye on her, and for a religious woman, she was not easily shaken. Thank fuck. When she'd told him that about herself, he thought maybe he had misheard. Why on earth would the Fates match a rounder like him with an angel like her?

Someone messed up, or maybe Derrick was right, and he got it all wrong. But nope. Weylin spent the last few days trailing her on two legs and four and he was more certain than ever. Gwendolyn Hoffer was supposed to be his.

"Weylin, can you take over? I'm going out for a bit with Leo to check our venue," Sheila called, breaking his train of thought.

He blinked, gaze shooting right over to where Gwen was pouring her next drink. She didn't even bother to glance at him. Shit. What was wrong with him? Did she find him unattractive? Too burly? Maybe she just didn't go for redheads.

Sad and dejected, he walked over to where the two females worked, staying on the opposite side of the bar. He just didn't trust himself to be any closer to her than that.

"Yep, I got it," he replied softly.

He sat down on a barstool and watching Gwen with a steady gaze. She glanced at him. Barely. It might have been a trick of the light. But he thought he saw her brown eyes widen for a moment. His Dire Wolf hummed with approval. Maybe she was aware of him on some level, at least. Even if she'd been doing her best to act like the other day hadn't happened.

He'd practically spent the entire day with her. After a friend of the Pack set him up with an established U-drive account, it was nothing at all to wait for her to order a car. He'd been surprised at the destination, but it did not matter. He would've driven her to Timbuktu if that was where she wanted to go.

She didn't know it, of course, but the feisty female was safe as could be with him. The fact she seemed to relax in his presence after some initial awkwardness warmed the beast within him. She hadn't expected more from him than a ride, but when he walked her inside and voiced his intentions to stay with her, she seemed grateful.

Poor thing, having to go through all that alone. He didn't know how she did it. Being born in a Pack meant you had people with you to back you up, bolster you, and offer support whether you wanted it or not. It was a choice sure, but Gwendolyn did not have that option.

Now she does. We'll be her Pack, his Wolf inserted.

His mind kept wandering back to that day, and he wondered what he'd done wrong to make her keep her distance ever since. Maybe Weylin had been too much, forcing his company on her by waiting in the hallway while Gwendolyn went inside Pop's room. Or perhaps, he hadn't done enough. The not knowing was eating at him, and the Wolf was getting antsy.

He didn't mean to eavesdrop, he couldn't help but overhear the doctor's prognosis. It was not good, but the older man was comfortable at least. No pain, that was what she'd begged, and Weylin's Wolf had raged at that.

"*Well?*" Gwen's soft voice asked the doctor, and Weylin heard the plea behind her words.

"*No change, Ms. Hoffer. He is comfortable for now, but the most recent scan showed a series of minor strokes. It is highly unlikely Mr. Hoffer will get out of bed again. I am very sorry,*" the doctor stated.

"*Oh no. Poor Pop,*" she'd murmured, tears in her voice.

Weylin had heard all he could take without moving into action. In half a second, he was beside her, wrapped his arm around her waist, and miracle of miracles, she'd leaned into him for support. The doctor waited for her to nod, and she did, then he went ahead and explained the test results in more detail.

He was so fucking relieved when she didn't back up or push him away. In fact, her tiny hand latched onto his as she allowed herself to rest against him. Taking comfort in his body was a gift he never expected, and fuck was it beautiful.

"Thank you, doctor," she had said when the man had finished his long speech.

Weylin had tried to listen to his words, but being so close to her had filled his senses. After hearing the news about her grandfather's condition, Gwendolyn had a moment of pure despair that was so heartbreaking all he could do was hold her while she cried.

Seeing her so upset was super hard, but hearing her plead with someone made him want to kill things. Lucky for the doctor, the man had been gentle when explaining their standard of care was to ensure all patients were very comfortable as they transitioned from this stage of life to the next.

Afterward, she sat by her grandfather, read to him. She cared for him and spent some time with the staff as well. Weylin waited in the hall, not wanting to intrude, but he heard everything, and his heart swelled with respect and affection for this intriguing woman.

Strong. Passionate. Loyal woman. Soft heart. Good heart.

They'd stayed a couple of hours, and when she was finished, he'd led the way back to his SUV, allowing the silence to envelop them like a safety blanket in the vehicle. The emotional and physical toll of seeing someone you loved suffer that way was unthinkable to him.

Dire Wolf Shifters lived very long lives, and illness rarely played a part. After a moment, his Gwendolyn with the pretty brown eyes had turned to him and thanked him—*him, Weylin Scott, newly reformed playboy who no one takes seriously*—for just being there with her. Like that was a hardship.

His heart thudded at the memory, and his Wolf bayed like a wild thing inside him.

"I'm so sorry for what you are going through, Gwendolyn. I know my opinion might not mean anything to you, but I think you're an incredible person. You care so much, sweetheart. I have never met anyone like you. And, this might not seem like much, but I am here for you if you need a hand, or a shoulder, or an ear, or anything at all."

He thought for sure he'd blown it. His Wolf was about to chew him a new asshole, but then she smiled through her tears. It was one of those tentative ones, watery, and kind of trembly. But maybe that was why it struck him like lightning.

Precious. Fleeting. Honest. Gift.

It was a moment he would never forget. Even now, he coveted it, cradling the memory to his heart and mind. Burying it deep so no one could ever take it from him.

"Thank you, Weylin. But you're wrong, it does mean a lot. You don't seem like the kind of guy who makes promises like that to just anyone, and I am touched, even if maybe I don't deserve them."

"What do you mean?"

"Despite what you saw, I'm not especially good or anything. It's just, he's my Pop."

"We can agree to disagree on you being especially good. Now, wanna go grab something to eat with me?"

He'd asked her to get food with him, even held his breath, waiting for her answer. Thank fuck, Gwendolyn had said yes. Driving an hour out of his way to feed her hot dogs from a famous hole in the wall grill that'd been serving the same deep fried dogs for over seventy-five years was fun.

She had scoffed at first, doubting any hot dog was worth the ride, but after her first bite, the girl was hooked. Damn, she was special. He had never had so much fun with a woman. She was even cute when she belched behind her napkin after she had polished off her third hot dog loaded with house-made relish and a tall, cold birch beer.

Gwen had been mortified until he let one rip out

his mouth, then she just laughed till she almost fell out of her chair. Afterward, they shared a huge slice of cherry pie, covered in real whipped cream, and then he brought her to the roadhouse to get ready for work.

Fun woman. Sexy, too.

CHAPTER 8

Everything had been going along just fine. Or so he'd thought. But overnight, something had changed. Gwendolyn had started avoiding him in earnest after that day. He felt raw and confused, his Dire Wolf, too.

Weylin hated to admit it, but he was a little bit butt hurt by the whole thing. Fuck, he didn't know how to do this. What she needed was someone with patience and understanding, but what the Fates stuck her with was him.

Weylin was OG love 'em and leave 'em type. He never had a serious relationship, flitting from bed to bed like a bee flying from flower to flower. At least he hadn't bedded any of their staff.

Oh, he'd had some minor flirtations with one or

two waitresses. But that was as far as it went. Even he knew not to shit where he ate.

Then there was the biggest impediment to his pursuing Gwendolyn, and that was the fact she was human. How he was going to get over that obstacle was a mystery to all, him included.

Weylin was a damn monster. These days, he was barely keeping his animal under control. It was way too soon for any normal to understand, but Gwendolyn Hoffer had already burrowed her way into Weylin's untried heart. Bottom line was he never felt this way about a woman before.

Warm. Fuzzy. Possessive. And yes, horny as fuck.

But it was more than that. He was curious about her. Wanted to learn what made her tick. He just had to get near her first, but she'd bolstered her defenses and was locked up tighter than Fort Knox.

It was hell on his nerves. He felt as smooth and suave as a pimple-faced virgin at the school prom whenever he was around Gwen. This was not his usual MO, for fuck's sake.

Weylin had his share of hot women. But not one of them held a candle to Gwen. Now that he had met his mate, they were just bodies in the dark. He had been open and honest with them, of course. He was Wolf, not a dog.

Dire Wolf Shifters never stayed in one place long enough to form permanent attachments. Until now. Hell, when Derrick had announced his intentions to settle down in one spot, plant roots, Weylin had initially balked.

Note to self: Send the Alpha a beef jerky bouquet and a thank you card.

Well, if he claimed his mate, maybe he would. For now, he would keep that notion under wraps. Derrick was being too much of a cockblocker to deserve any meaty goodness.

Second note to self: Send myself a beef jerky bouquet because I am awesome, and I am gonna win my mate.

Yeah, that was more like it! Weylin could not be more grateful for his Pack setting up shop in this little slip of a town in New Jersey. This place had presented him with something to work for. A goal. His mate.

Mine.

Gwen's natural strawberry scent reached his nostrils, and his lips flexed in an easy smile as he breathed her in. So tempting. Sweet. Fresh.

"Ready," she said, excitement ringing in her voice.

"All done?" he asked as she finished pouring the last drink into a martini glass.

It was a twist on a lemon drop martini made with

a brand new local label, Crescent Moon Gin. It was a new branch of the Bite label owned and operated by Mason Lane, a member of the Macconwood Wolf Pack. Good people. Good Shifters. And the guy made fantastic spirits far as the Dire Wolf Pack was concerned.

"Yep. All done. Lemme know what you think," Gwen replied, biting her lip as he sipped drink after drink, washing his mouth out with water between sips.

Weylin was a consummate professional. Fated mate or not, he had to take his job as a co-owner of Serious Moonlight, *er*, seriously. He opened his senses before each sip, allowing the depth of the flavors, the essence of the alcohol, and the ratio of sweet, tart, and bitter to filter through as he tried each one.

Holy, Fuck. The woman was a rockstar.

Mine.

"Shit."

"Shit?" she asked, frowning hard.

"No, no," he blurted. "I meant it like, shit, girl, these are fantastic!" he told her with a grin.

Just like that, his sassy sweet Gwendolyn lit up before him. He'd be a liar if he said it meant nothing to him, that way she had of glowing at the smallest of compliments. He'd bet she wasn't used to them, and damn, but he wanted to change that. She deserved compliments. Lots of them.

"Really?" she asked, her lips turned up in a mirror image of his own expression.

Weylin nodded, his heart warming at her obvious pleasure. He liked she was so happy when he complimented her. Wanted to see what else he could say or do to bring that look of joy to her face, that hint of radiance to her caramel eyes.

"Truly. You nailed them!"

"Yes! Okay, so do you think I can handle the back bar tonight?" Gwen asked.

The back bar was Lucy's usual haunt, and since Gwen was filling in for the Alpha fem, Weylin did not have an issue with it. She'd been tending bar the last three nights beside Sheila and the she-Wolf had nothing but glowing reports on how the curvy little normal had handled herself. Apparently, her sassy mouth was a source of amusement with the females of the Pack.

Takes one to know one, he mused. Not that he'd be saying that out loud. Those Pack females scared the shit out of him. Any sane man would say the same, of that he was certain.

"Think you're ready to go it alone? It's Saturday, you know. Our busiest night," he told her.

"I'm ready, and you know I need the tips," Gwen replied, no guile in her voice.

He knew she was working hard to pay for her Pop's care. Hell, he wished he could just give her the money, but it was too soon for that. He tried hinting at a loan and she damn near turned to ice. He read between the lines. Gwen would not take any hand-outs from him.

"Alright. You can take the lead in the back bar. I'll be checking in on you from time to time, but don't be afraid to call out if you need something."

"Okay, but if you come back here, who will handle the front?" she asked.

"Saturday, remember? Me and Cole will both be at the front bar, but I'm manager tonight. If there is an issue, I will deal with it."

She had her hands on her hips but was listening to everything he said. If he didn't know any better, he would think she was a Shifter the way she practically growled at him with her normal little voice. She had grit, that one. Grit and sass, and fuck, was it sexy!

"You'll be keeping tabs on me. Got it," she said. "I won't let you down."

"You couldn't if you tried," Weylin whispered and rubbed the back of his neck.

Tonight was going to be a long one. He probably needed to let the Wolf out before the crowd started coming in. Weylin was shifting into his Wolf every night, but he was staying outside her room and that was not the same as running.

The animal needed to let off some steam. Usually, his choices were to shift and run in the woods or find some woman to fuck when he got this antsy. He didn't want anyone but Gwen, and she was nowhere near ready for physical intimacy, so shifting to his monster won out.

"Oh, my shirt came in," Gwen told him with a grin that stopped him in his tracks.

She was so damn pretty. Her hair was down, and curls were raining down her back and shoulders, so bouncy and sexy. He was dying to feel them between his fingers. Wondered if they were coarse or silky. He would bet on the latter, but damn, wouldn't he love to find out for sure?

His attention was snagged by Gwen as she held up the teeny weeny excuse for a t-shirt that Sheila had ordered her. Weylin frowned hard.

Fuck.

There he was, hoping he wouldn't have to smack

anyone upside the head tonight, but it looked like that plan was flying right out the window. The woman was fine as fuck in baggy tees and cotton pants. But he had forgotten all about the Serious Moonlight uniform—*if you could call it that.*

Thank you very much, Sheila. Fuck.

"Hey, you don't have to look like that. It will fit me," Gwen retorted.

Her posture had gone ramrod straight, and the scent coming off her was bitter, like she was angry or hurt. Fuck. She was obviously mistaking his momentary pause for something it wasn't. But that was all his fault. He should have explained better.

"Hang on a second, Gwen—"

"No need. I understand by your expression what you are thinking, but let me tell you something, people come in all shapes and sizes."

"Gwen, I think you misunderstood, and I know that's my fault, but if you just let me—"

The woman was not letting him get a word in edge wise, and fuck, it was difficult for him to stay focused. Her eyes were bright, and her hair was flying as she waved her hands around as she spoke in true New Jersey fashion.

"I know the shirt looks small, but Sheila said it stretches. And yes, I realize I am a big girl, but that is no one's business, but mine. I have tended bar before, and let me tell you something, Mr. Body Beautiful, my boobs usually detract from my belly, so you don't have to worry about me. I will do just fine with your customers. The rest of me will be behind the bar. I won't embarrass you or the business," she said each word with a hushed fury that both startled and turned him on.

Damn, but she was feisty. Gorgeous in her fury, too, but she had it all wrong.

"Gwen, I gotta tell you, I have no idea what you are talking about," he growled.

"Listen up, because I will only say this once. Words have power, and I believe in being kind to my body and my mind. Now, I realize I don't look like you all, but can I help it if I wasn't blessed with whatever superior physical genes your entire friend circle was blessed with? I mean, I have never seen so many tall, muscular, good-looking people in one place in my life. But that doesn't mean I will shame you when I put on the uniform—"

"Hang on a second," he pleaded louder.

His heart was pounding, the Wolf clawing at hm. Fuck! He fucked this all up. Weylin felt like was about to explode, but wait—*did she say?*

"You think I'm good-looking?"

That little doozy seemed to stop her tirade, and Weylin's grin grew wider. Her arousal teased his senses, adding even more sweetness to her natural strawberry scent. Weylin's chest rumbled with his beast as he watched her like the predator he was.

"Oh, like you need me to tell you that you're hot. Fish for compliments somewhere else, buster. Besides, I heard all about you from the waitstaff. You're a regular heartbreaker, aren't you?" she replied, hands on those damn delightful hips of hers.

What? Shit. The staff was talking shit about him. Well, that sucked.

"Gwendolyn, I don't know what you heard, but I never fooled around with someone who didn't know the deal, alright? And never with any of the staff. Besides, I already told you, that's behind me now," Weylin said, narrowing his eyes at her.

"Whatever," she replied.

She placed her hands on her hips, and fuck if that didn't emphasize her sexy little curves. Her brown eyes seemed to glow amber, spitting fire as her temper fluctuated. Sassy, sweet, and so damn pretty his heart was liable to stop if he kept on staring. Call him a glutton for punishment, cause he simply could not look away.

Her chest lifted as she sucked in a deep breath,

and he closed his eyes. The longing he felt was fucking painful. But if he failed at every other thing, he had to at least clear the air between them.

"Just for the record, Gwen, I wasn't staring at you because I thought the shirt was too small. I was staring at you because the thought of anyone else seeing you in that is making me lose my damn mind," he ground out, gritting his teeth to try to hold in his animal's snarl.

The Wolf was damn near crazed with the idea he had hurt her. Even unintentionally, it ripped him up inside to know he had caused her any bit of hurt.

"I'm sorry that was unprofessional and unkind," Gwendolyn replied, eyes downcast.

Well, shit. He didn't want her feeling bad or anything. Fuck. he was not cut out for this. She was better off without him.

Grrrr.

"No need for apologies. I'm the fuckup here. You are gonna rock the shit out of that uniform, baby," he murmured, the endearment natural as it slipped from his lips.

He was always calling her baby or sweetheart or something cute cause he thought she was just that. Cute as a dumpling and ten times as tasty.

Mine. Want. Grr.

Ha, you don't have to say that," she started.

Her cheeks were turning pink, so he knew she liked the compliment. Good. That was good, right? His animal let him breathe easier, but he was still scratching to get out.

Fuck.

Weylin needed fresh air. He needed space.

"Alright, um, why don't you go on and get ready? I will meet you at the back bar later on, okay?"

Weylin waited for her nod before letting go of the breath he'd been holding. She was still frowning, and he felt like a total piece of shit. The woman was so damn beautiful it hurt to look at her and not touch her, but she didn't know he felt like that. How could she when he wasn't even allowed to tell her?

Fuck. Fuck. FUCK.

He left her there, hauling ass to the side door down the hallway. He had to slow his breathing. He felt his Wolf clawing inside, and it hurt like hell. There was not much time before shit got busy, but Weylin had to make it outside, to the woods at the end of the lot. Then he could shift and run and get rid of some of his animal's angst. A sound brought his head up, and he turned with a snarl on his lips.

"You alright?" Cole asked, hands raised, and Weylin shook his head.

"Nah. I am far fucking from it," he growled.

"Look, you need to relax. I think Derrick is right. Forget the normal, man. Maybe you should go out for a ride or something. Grab your bike and take off for a few months?"

His Pack mate stared at him like he was fucking crazy, and Weylin wanted to punch him in the face. Asshole. Forget her? Was he insane? Gwendolyn was ingrained in his very soul. Cole and Derrick could just fuck right off. He was not giving her up. He just needed a plan to woo her, that was all.

"She's not just some normal, Cole," he growled. "Gwendolyn is my fated mate, okay? I felt it the first time I saw her. My Wolf knows it. I'll lose my mind without her, man. She is it for me," he confessed to his Pack mate.

Cole scowled, hands on his hips. Weylin knew what he was thinking. It was the same thing Derrick had said. They finally had a place of their own after wandering around the world for decades without roots or ties.

It was no simple thing. The Dire Wolf Pack had settled down, and they did not want to risk it. Outing what he was to a normal was always gonna be risky. Even worse, if she rejected him, his beast would go mad, and Derrick would have to put him down.

Fuck.

His Alpha did not want that on his plate, and he could not blame him. Neither did Weylin. But what choice did he have?

His sensitive ears picked up on the sounds of the band arriving. They were a Shifter group, all women, and they usually packed the house. Sure, the bar's customers tended to be mostly supes, though the odd human came in from time to time.

He could hear them loading their instruments onto the stage. Other sounds filtered through to where he and Cole stood by that side door. Brock shouted orders from the kitchen, the nighttime wait staff was slowly filing in, and Thor, another Pack mate, had taken his place by the door as the bouncer for the night.

It was just another Saturday night, and Serious Moonlight promised to be packed.

"I can't pretend to know what you're going through, man," Cole added. "But maybe just take it day by day."

"Yeah," Weylin nodded, clapping the male on the shoulder as he walked past.

Not like he could take the days two at a time,

anyway. Slow and steady won the race. But Gwendolyn wasn't just some race he wanted to win. She wasn't a challenge he needed to notch his bedpost. She was his whole damn future. For a Dire Wolf who never took things seriously before, and enjoyed living in the fast lane, slow and steady was a helluva change.

"So, shift if you need to. I will cover you for a while. But bro, is she worth it?" Cole asked before he walked away.

"Fuck yeah," Weylin replied automatically.

As if on cue, Gwendolyn entered the hall, dressed in the bar uniform. Her brown eyes found his across the way, and he was struck dumb.

Holy hell.

She must have brought her own ripped up jeans because they hugged her curves like a second skin, accentuating the dip of her waist and flare of her hips. That little cotton t-shirt with the neon pink Serious Moonlight logo splashed across the front didn't look like it had a prayer of containing her ample bosoms for the duration.

Strategically ripped and cut low in the front, exposing the trim of the sexy lace bra she had on underneath. It was enough to make his mouth water. A growl left his throat at the mere thought of anyone else looking at her this way, but he had no right to be so damn protective.

The truth of that statement did nothing to settle his beast down. Hell, she deserved compliments and stares. She was gorgeous. Weylin shouldn't be worried about anything. Whatever woman magic females used when it came to turning men into obsessive nincompoops, she'd done her bit alright. Weylin was a fool for her and right then, he did not care who knew it.

His eyes ate her up as she slowly walked confidently across the floor, high-heeled boots on her feet making a *clack clack clack* sound as she went. The beat was in time with his heavily pounding heart, not to mention the thumping erection below his belt. He'd never seen such a tempting woman in all his life.

She ducked her head down, as if steeling herself, then found his gaze once more. The smile she gave him then was bright, and he felt one echoing across his face. Lifting her arms, she did a little spin for him, and he grinned even wider.

Heartbreaker.

Damn, she was sexy as fuck with that little strip of skin around her navel peeking out as her raised arms lifted the tight shirt. Her confidence and obvious enjoyment made her even more attractive.

"Holy hell. Little normal is smokin' hot!" Cole mumbled from beside him, followed by an, "Ooof!"

Whatever. It was only a little punch. Weylin tried not to grin as the fucker gasped. Cole went in for a punch, but Weylin blocked him easily, all without turning his head. He twisted the man's arm, and Cole whimpered.

"Ouch!"

"Fuck off, Cole."

"Stop staring at her so we can have a decent fight," grumbled his Pack mate.

"Not on your life," Weylin grunted.

If he had the choice, he would never stop staring at her. Gwendolyn frowned over her shoulder at the two men before walking to the back bar. What a pleasant view it was, watching her butt sway from side to side in her new gear. The woman was killing him, but he had a plan now.

Slow and steady. Fuck what his Pack mates thought. Gwendolyn Hoffer was going to be his.

Mine.

CHAPTER 9

It was only eleven, and the place was jampacked. The band was really rocking, and she had to hand it to them, they were the best all-female group she'd ever seen, except for maybe clips of the Go-Go's on YouTube. She'd been juggling customers between sets, and so far, so good.

"How are you doing back here?" Weylin asked.

Gwen froze from where she was bent over, retrieving more longnecks to fill the coolers lining the back of the bar. Beer and shots had been the standard so far.

"Great!" she said too brightly as she spun around to face him.

Weylin Scott. Sexy, confident, growly, redheaded alpha male. Great, there she went, waxing poetic on the guy again. The man had been taking up way too much headspace lately.

"Awesome, Gwen. So, what do you think?"

Did he have to be so damn cute? She wrang out a rag over the sink, and shrugged, determined to keep things light. Maybe if she hadn't been such a hardass about that promise she'd made, she wouldn't feel this way.

Ugh.

It was one thing to vow to save yourself for marriage because you believed in love. Quite another to hold on to that vow because you were betrayed by a boy you had no business dating, anyway. If only she could go back in time and warn her college self that bitterness was a joy killer. Holding on to one thing because a bad thing had happened was probably not a good idea.

But that was what she'd done. Held on to her virginity, like it was some prize. Now she was a thirty year old virgin with a crush on a playboy bartender who would likely laugh at her ignorance of the most basic bedroom shenanigans. What a mess!

And telling him she wouldn't sleep with him? Why had she done that? He probably thought she was just playing hard to get and saw the whole thing as some game! This was so messed up.

"Um, you were right," she said, realizing she had to reply. "The bar is really crowded, and I can see why. The band is fantastic. The food is even better."

"And the drinks are flowing from the fingers of a pretty and expert mixologist at the back bar," he added with a grin.

"What?" Gwen asked, shock making her eyebrows arch.

"Seriously, some of your customers are complimenting your skills."

"Yeah, right?" she snorted but couldn't hide her pleasure at the unexpected compliment.

"Why shouldn't they? There's nothing like getting a good cold drink from the hands of a pretty professional bartender."

"Compliments will get you nowhere," she mumbled.

Good thing the music was loud and bar full, otherwise he might have heard the catch in her breath when she spoke. It was just so unfair. If only she knew more about the opposite sex. Maybe then she could have just casually flirted back with him, and ignored all the butterflies and fighter jets flapping against her insides.

"Don't I know it, Gwen," he replied, but his eyes were all glittery and his gaze direct.

Shivers.

The man gave her chills. Gwendolyn had worked in some pretty popular places when she was in school in Manhattan, and in her opinion, Serious Moonlight could rival any of the bars and restaurants in the big city.

It was just that good. Of course, there was also the eye candy. She had never seen so many gorgeous people in one place. Of course, no one could hold a candle to Weylin. Not that she cared.

Liar.

Whatever. Gwen knew she wasn't in his league, and she even understood him kissing her meant nothing to him. It couldn't. She rolled her eyes and went back to stocking the coolers, but he took the case of beer from her and went to work as another customer called for her attention.

She smiled at the young man, nodding as he ordered a round of tequila shots, and went about setting them up. She fully expected Weylin to leave, but he didn't. Her skin tingled with nerves every time she brushed her arm against his. It was close quarters, but it wasn't like she could order him to leave. He was her boss, after all.

Every cell seemed aware of him, and it was wreaking havoc with her nervous system. Maybe it was the atmosphere, but every time she got a look at the big sexy redhead, Gwendolyn had the naughtiest visions of him trapping her in his arms and nibbling on her skin.

Yes, please.

No. Down, girl.

Lord, this was so not good for her. She knew better than to be tempted by sins of the flesh, but holy crap was he gorgeous. Yes, he flirted, and she appreciated she was just one of many females following him around with her eyes like a lost puppy. But a girl could dream, right?

"Tips good?" he asked, coming behind the bar and lifting the case of beer easily for her.

"Uh, yeah. Better than I expected," she told him.

Truthfully, they were awesome. If she made this much on one Saturday, then she'd have the next payment for Hope Springs sooner than she thought. That was good. After all, that was why she was there. To pay for Pop's care. Not drool over a man.

"That's terrific. I'll finish filling these for you and I will check the hard stuff too, okay?"

"Yep. Thanks," she replied tightly.

Get a grip, Gwenny.

"Here you go," Gwendolyn said, returning to the bar and lining up the six shots of tequila, complete with a couple of saltshakers and six slices of lime in front of her customer.

"No, baby, here you go," the young flirtatious male retorted, pushing one shot back her way.

"Oh, thank you, but I don't drink hard liquor," she replied, shaking her head but smiling to soften the blow.

"You have to. It's like bartending rules, if a customer buys you a shot, you drink," he said, and there was something in his eyes she did not quite like.

Gwen smiled and shook her head, politely refusing the drink. The man had some buddies who were finishing their own shots, slamming the glasses back down on the table. The rowdy group of guys lined up next to him, chanting for her to *drink drink drink.*

"I'll buy this round, how about that? You all have a good night," she said, trying to keep the customers happy.

"I said drink," he snarled, grabbing her wrist when she would have turned around.

Gwendolyn winced under the man's surprise strength, and before she could do more than open her mouth, Weylin was there. He vaulted over the bar gracefully and had the man by the throat faster than she could blink.

Her wrist was suddenly released, and she staggered back, hardly realizing she'd been pulling to get away. Oh, but Weylin looked furious. His nostrils flared and eyes glittered like emerald ice as he lifted the man up to eye level. Totally in control, he dragged the jerk closer and whispered something in a voice way too low for Gwen to hear.

"You alright here?"

Gwen turned around and yelped at the image Thor had made beside her. The man was huge, even bigger than Weylin, with a shaved head and a dozen tattoos that she could see.

"Did that guy hurt you?" he asked.

All she could do was shake her head. The guy was a prick, but he hadn't hurt her. He was young, and a little buzzed, clearly trying to show off in front of his friends.

Thor's eyes were dark as midnight, and just as scary, she thought as he nodded over her head. When she turned, it was to see Weylin dragging the handsy jerk and his buddies out of the bar. Anger coursed through her. He didn't have to do that!

She would have been fine. Maybe. But anyway,

he had no right to just swoop in and treat her like some dang damsel in distress.

"Hey, Thor?" Gwen shouted as the man turned to leave.

She knew she shouldn't be doing this. She should leave well enough alone. But it bothered her that Weylin thought her so weak. She could have handled that idiot customer. Plus, she didn't need him messing with her brain this way.

Weylin was her friend. That was all. He didn't get to go all protective boyfriend on her for no reason. Besides, she didn't inspire that kind of reaction in men. Besides, that whole thing with her uniform earlier just confused her even more. She couldn't afford to think things that were not real. Especially since she kinda sorta maybe had a developed the tiniest crush on the guy.

Fine. She had the hots for him. The full-blown, thinking about him all the time despite certain vows she'd made as a teenager kind of hots. Shit. Gwen needed to clear the air for sure.

"Yeah?" the big man asked.

"Can you watch the bar for a moment? I need to tell Weylin something."

"Uh. I really don't like talking to people, Gwen, you see, I'm more a bouncer—"

But she was already taking off the tiny waist apron she had on and walking after Weylin. He'd gone through the front door, so it was going to take her a moment to get through the crowd. NO. She could get to the back lot faster through the side kitchen door.

Good plan.

"Thanks, Thor!" she called back, not even listening to what he said.

Her heart was pounding, and she did not know why, but it was like her whole being was focused on getting outside. Getting to him. Right now.

Once she stepped into the night, Gwen was taken in by how dark it seemed. The neon sign broke up the deep purple skies, and the air seemed tense, full of mystery and magic.

Oh what fanciful nonsense, she mused, shaking her head.

"Weylin?" she called softly, walking around the building itself.

It was dark with the odd light here and there, but Gwen couldn't see anything. She listened a moment, hearing strange popping noises, and followed them to the end of the parking lot.

"Weylin?"

———

Weylin's Dire Wolf was scratching at his insides. He needed to change into his fur before he fucking lost it in front of the entire bar. Seeing that bastard's hand on her wrist had damn near made him lose it completely.

Good thing the asshole punk was a Shifter because even in pulling his punch, Weylin had clocked him harder than he'd meant once he had him outside. Little fucker deserved it. What kind of man tried to force a drink or anything at all on a woman? Well, he and his buddies had learned their lesson after tonight.

But even that didn't do much to calm his beast. Asshole punk Shifter kid should have known better than to do that kind of thing to a female. And not just any female, but a human one. It was all he could manage not to change inside and tear the asshole a new, *er*, asshole.

That would have broken every Shifter rule there was, including the main one which was absolutely no exposing themselves to humans. Gwen was a human. She knew nothing about him or his kind, and so far, he had yet to convince Derrick to allow him to tell the woman who would be his mate the truth about himself.

Weylin was in a tight spot. How was he going to convince her he was serious about her? He only kissed Gwendolyn that one time, and her consequent smacking of his face was not an encouraging sign she was meant to be his. At least, that was what the Alpha thought.

He believed Weylin was jumping the gun. But this was no mistake. Regardless of Derrick's expectations that Weylin would move on to the next female as he'd done before, he knew that was so not happening. It was different with Gwen. She was it for him.

Weylin felt it down to his marrow. The Wolf inside him knew it, too. He just had to stay the course. But it was not easy. With her religious upbringing and moral compass, and the promise she made to herself regarding her—*Christ, Weylin could hardly think the word without going cross-eyed*—virginity, Gwendolyn was skittish around him, to say the least.

Every time he thought of the line she'd drawn in the sand between them, he wanted to howl at the moon like a wild thing. His desire for her was fierce, but the tenderness he felt, that was the real surprise.

She needed patience, so he would give her that. But that didn't mean it was easy.

Being near her, smelling her, seeing her every day was the best part of his world right now. Also, the worst. How could he be so close and not tell her she was his? It was torture having to keep how he felt hidden, like a dark, dirty secret when it was none of those things.

Sure, this was new and scary. But from what he knew of her already, she was fierce and brave. Strong woman. Beautiful, loyal, and brave. She'd made a vow to save herself for marriage, and he wanted to honor that vow.

Weylin knew she was meant for him. Hell, he would marry her right now if he thought she would say yes. The idea of spending forever with her warmed his heart, made his blood pump faster.

Too fast. She's human. Slow it down.

He was stuck between a rock and a hard place—*a very hard place*—waiting for her to give him a sign she was interested. Add to that his Alpha's order to stay away from the human and bam! You had one very frustrated, whiny, pining Dire Wolf.

Weylin felt like he was being torn apart. He took his shirt in one hand, ripping it over his head. The side door by the kitchen slammed, but he paid it no mind. Brock was always sneaking off for a moment of silence when he was in the kitchen. The Wolf was a master chef, but he could be a damn lunatic about how he ran his ship.

By the time he heard who had really followed him outside, it was too late.

"Weylin? Oh my God! You're a-a WEREWOLF!"

Fuck. Shit. No. GWEN!

"Awoooooooooooooooooooooooooooooo!"

CHAPTER 10

"Is she alright?" Gwen did not recognize the man's voice.

"She looks like she's coming around," came a soft reply, maybe from Tracey.

"What the fuck did you do, asshole? I told you to stay away. She's human, for fuck's sake!" Derrick's angry voice reached her ears.

"It's not my fault, man. Some guy grabbed her, a Shifter dick, at the bar, and I lost it. Needed to change," Weylin murmured, his voice sounding all gritty and sexy.

"Guys, shh!" Lucy whisper-screamed and Gwen wanted to smile.

Instead, she closed her eyes tight.

"What happened?" she asked, and her mouth felt like she had just eaten a wad of cotton.

Her memories came back slowly, replaying in her mind. Earlier, Gwen had been going through the list of signature cocktails, practicing them for tonight. It was her first time handling the back bar alone, and she'd been so excited.

Saturday nights were reportedly jampacked, and she had been looking forward to the tips. She ran her hands over her body. She had on ripped jeans and a tee, so she was already in uniform. That was right. She'd been working the back bar, and it was going well.

Gwen blinked her eyes open, slowly at first, and warm light filled her vision. Weylin had come to the back, was helping her restock. She had a customer. He wanted shots. He got a little mean, then Weylin jumped over the bar and –*what next?*

"She's waking up. Hey, Gwen. How are you feeling?" a petite blonde—*Lucy*—asked, helping Gwen to a sitting position.

Her mind was hazy. She turned and looked at the two huge men in the room. One she recognized as her new boss, Derrick Rand. The other was him. Weylin Scott. The redheaded hottie who'd been filling her dreams with naughty visions and causing several sleepless nights over the past week.

He wasn't wearing a shirt, and his rippling muscles were a huge distraction to her addled brain. Wowza. He had a bunch of sexy tribal tattoos criss-crossing his body that Gwen hadn't known about. Why would she? Not like she had that kind of rela-tionship with him—or anyone since, *well*, ever.

"Ouch, my head," she mumbled as she pressed her feet firmly to the floor.

"Here, drink this," Lucy said, handing her a glass of ice cold cola.

"Thank you. Mm, that's sweet," she murmured.

"I figured the sugar and caffeine would help," Lucy, who was very pregnant, replied and shrugged.

"Oh, the bar, I should get back to work—"

"Honey, the bar is all closed. Everyone is home. Now you just take as long as you need," Lucy murmured.

The bar was closed? Crap. That must mean it was after three. Gwen closed her eyes and took a steadying breath. They were in Derrick's office again, and she was on the big couch he kept there. Still, she was starting to feel a little like a pinned butterfly.

"Do you all mind not staring?" she asked.

"Sorry," Lucy whispered, grinning at her for some reason.

"Gwendolyn, what do you remember about what happened?" Derrick asked.

"Um, I don't know. I was at the back bar. Tending it like Sheila taught me and keeping the crowd happy. Mostly beer tonight, but some shots too. Oh, Weylin helped restock the cooler. Then I think I, um, had a customer and I disagreed with him about something, maybe?" she said, searching his green eyes for clues.

She had only ever seen Weylin Scott looking cocky or earnest, but right then, he appeared concerned and a little freaked out. What the heck had happened?

"He wanted you to take a shot," Weylin inserted carefully.

"That's right. Tequila. Um, I don't drink hard liquor straight," she explained to Derrick. "It makes me sick. Especially, shots. I'm sorry, I know it is customary for bartenders to drink sometimes with customers—"

"That's alright, Gwen. You never have to drink if you don't want to," Derrick replied. "What else do you recall, if anything?" he pressed.

Lucy rose from her seated position and eyed her

man strangely. What the heck was going on here? Gwendolyn blinked, shaking her head to clear it. Oh boy, that was a mistake! She pressed her fingers to her temples.

"Ouch! Is this a bump?" she mumbled and pressed gently around the tender area.

"Fuck, Gwen. I am so sorry. You hit your head when you fell, and I wasn't fast enough," Weylin confessed, looking worried and sick as he gripped the back of his neck with one hand.

"I fainted?"

"Shut up, Weylin," Derrick growled, and for some reason, Gwen really did not like that at all.

"Hey, I don't mean to be out of line, but what is your problem, Derrick? Weylin just apologized for something that doesn't seem to be his fault, like at all. That customer grabbed my wrist, ouch, look, he even left a bruise! Weylin got me out of a tight situation, so why don't you give him a break?" she said, staring at the big man until it got uncomfortable.

Derrick's chest was rumbling, and she did not know why, but Gwen dropped her gaze. Weylin had stood up at this point, body tense as he moved between Gwen and Derrick. What the heck was going on?

"It's okay, Gwendolyn. He's just doing his job,"

Weylin murmured, tilting his head oddly and avoiding Derrick's glare.

What the heck?

"Wait," she said, turning back to Weylin. "I don't remember tripping. How did I fall? What happened?"

"Gwen, maybe you should take the night off—" Derrick said, but Lucy clamped her hand over his mouth.

"Baby, I have a craving for a cheesesteak. Take me to Tony's, would you?" she asked, rubbing her protruding belly and pouting at her man.

Gwendolyn felt sort of like a voyeur, watching the obvious chemistry between them. Even with her belly swollen with his baby, Derrick seemed to find her irresistible. Wasn't that something?

"Lucy, I am in the middle of something here," Derrick began in a growly voice that sorta scared Gwendolyn.

Lucy didn't seem to mind. In fact, the woman swayed closer to him. Weird. But it must be nice, Gwen mused.

Oh sure, Gwen talked a good game about being fine alone. After one lousy little heartbreak, she'd been hiding behind her promise to save herself for marriage. But that imaginary future husband was just that—*imaginary*.

Truth was, Gwendolyn never planned on finding a guy who could measure up to her book boyfriends. How could she? Folks thought Walt Disney was responsible for unhealthy expectations of what true love was supposed to be like, but she knew better.

That man had nothing on the romance writers of the world, especially the indies. There was nothing Gwen liked more than to find a brand new favorite author pioneer in the indie publishing world.

"Fine. I will take myself," Lucy growled, slapping her hands against the mountainous man's chest, and pushing him back.

He moved, too. Though Gwen was certain that was only because he wanted to. No way could a tiny thing like Lucy move that giant of hers. Lucy tossed her blonde hair over her shoulder and narrowed her eyes at Derrick before grabbing the keys off his desk.

With a sharp nod, she waved goodbye to Gwen with a wink, then stomped out of the office, big booty swaying as she went.

Uh oh.

"What? Dammit. No! Wait! Weylin, fix this!" Derrick snapped before running after Lucy. "Not the

Harley, Kitten, come on. We'll take the truck! It's better for the cubs!"

"Did he say cubs?" she turned her head and asked Weylin.

"Um, let's talk about what happened for a minute, then we will get into that," Weylin said, standing up.

He started rummaging through the cabinet behind Derrick's desk and pulled out a clean, black t-shirt with the bar's logo on it. Gwendolyn frowned at the loss of all those tattooed muscles, but she supposed it was for the better. After all, her adult life had been all about avoiding the kind of temptation a man like him presented.

"Look, I owe you an apology," he began, turning to face her as he pulled the shirt over his head.

Gwen gulped down a whimper as she faced his pure masculine perfection. Yeah, he had some scars on his pale skin, but they did nothing to deter from his male beauty. His tattoos were many and so intricate, the detail was just beyond anything she had ever seen. He was a living work of art, and Gwen's heart fluttered in response to that realization.

"Why do you owe me an apology?" she asked.

"I seem to put my foot in my mouth whenever I try with you. I keep giving you the wrong impression, Gwendolyn."

"How? When? I mean, we hardly know each other," she murmured, but even saying that felt wrong.

Ever since she wandered into *Serious Moonlight*, something about the place, the people, just seemed to call to her. Gwendolyn's world wasn't so big, she wasn't so lonely when she was with them. This strange group of beautiful people had made her feel like she belonged to something, even as dumb as that sounded, she realized she was right.

"Since day one, I've been keeping secrets."

"Secrets? Why?"

"All I wanted was to know you better, but you told me to stay away, and I just couldn't, beautiful—"

"Stop," she said, angry now that he was trying to play her. "You don't have to say things like that to me. Sheila is beautiful. Big as she is with her baby, Lucy is beautiful. Not me. At the most, I'm cute. It's fine though, I am happy being cute, but what does that have to do with why I woke up in here?" she asked, tucking her hair behind her ear.

"Maybe to some people you are cute, but I called you beautiful because you are to me, dammit," he growled, stepping forward and invading her space.

Eyes wide, she backed up instinctively. He was just so big. So much man. She could feel heat rolling off his body, warming her in the cramped office. Gwen gasped as her back met with the wall, but he'd already put his hands there, cushioning her from it.

"You scared the crap out of me, woman, fainting like that. Fuck, I've never been that scared," he mumbled.

"Sorry," she murmured, reaching out with shaky hands to touch him.

She was acting on instinct, and it was scary. She'd never touched a man like that, with long, slow strokes down his chest. She wanted to calm him, soothe him, but had no idea if it was right.

He sucked in a breath, then big, tall, too hand-some Weylin just shuddered. He closed his fiery emerald eyes, giving her a reprieve from their intensity, and leaned into her touch.

Dammit if she didn't miss the intensity of his stare almost immediately. Honestly, she loved being caught up in the emerald fire of his gaze. Then he pressed his forehead to hers in a gesture that felt like it meant something bigger than what it was, and her insides just melted.

What was happening? She should stop this, right? Pushing him away or slapping his face for presuming to touch her without permission, but her hands seemed frozen in place on his body, and wild horses couldn't pull her away.

There is something different about this one. Wait and see. Give him a chance.

Gwen didn't know what to do, or how to quiet the voice in her head she attributed to the naughty angel on her shoulder. So, she let go of all feigned control, and just let it happen.

Yeah, she had very little experience with men, and whatever she might have promised herself, it looked like her body had other ideas. Desires and needs were flaring to life. Secret hidden ones she hardly ever expected to feel at all.

It was scary and wonderful, and for once in her life, she felt like the heroine in one of those romance novels she loved. Weylin smelled so good. That woodsy scent she'd started associating with him alone seemed brighter now, stronger with him so close.

Weylin's eyes seemed to glow in the dimly lit room, and for one moment, she swore she saw swirls of something else deep within the emerald depths. Like there was another consciousness present in his gaze, and this one watched her, too. The idea should have frightened her, but all it did was kindle her desire.

Gwendolyn shivered, her breasts flattened against his chest as he leaned down. She saw something outside. Just before she fainted. It was right there in her memory. Something impossible. Scary even.

Fur. Fangs. Claws.

The sounds of bones cracking and tendons snapping ringing in her ears.

Impossible.

It had to be a trick of the mind. Gwen's breath caught as she tried to force the memory, but Weylin was leaning in closer, so much closer. His body felt good against hers. He was hot, hard, and heavy. She was hypnotized, confounded, and desperate for whatever came next.

Please, oh please, let there be more.

"Everyone keeps telling me to wait, to give you time. But I don't think I can wait another minute," he murmured in a voice so low she hardly heard him.

"For what?" she whispered her reply, holding her breath as anticipation reached a crescendo.

"This."

Then he was kissing her, and Gwen could not think at all. Well, nothing except, oooh, was he good at this. So good. So much better than that first time.

"Gwen," he moaned her name, angling her head as he deepened the kiss. "Christ, you're sweet."

Lust glazed eyes blinked down at her, and she knew her own stare must have looked just as dreamy. Weylin smiled that slow panty-melting grin of his before capturing her mouth again. His tongue delved between her lips, and she moaned her response.

Hot boy. Sexy boy. Turning her head. Making her feel.

He ground his hips into hers and she felt him there, in that place she had neglected so long. Yearning built and built and built until she was moving with him.

He's making a fool of you. Using you. That is what he's doing—No! Shhh!

Gwen shushed that nasty little voice in her head and held on to the moment. To Weylin. To the man right in front of her. His eyes opened, the green was so bright they were neon and a shiver raced up her spine. He could see straight into her soul with those eyes. And he was, wasn't he? Seeing all her secret needs and wants. All her hidden desires and fantasies.

Suddenly, her memory came plowing back into her brain like thunder and with her two hands on his chest, Gwendolyn pushed, forcing Weylin away from her. Fuck. She missed his heat, his scent, his strength. But no. This could not be. Horror, confusion, and dread filled her.

"What is it? Did I hurt you?" he asked, baffled.

In her mind's eye, she saw the memory she'd tried to block out. Weylin naked, stopped over by the edge of the forest. His body bent, face contorted with pain as he broke apart.

Skin tore, bones snapped, and fur sprouted where it shouldn't be possible. His body shifted and changed from the most handsome man she had ever seen, the gentle giant she had grown to care about, and lust for, to something out of a nightmare or a dream.

Weylin Scott was no ordinary man. Gwendolyn's breath caught in her throat as she raised her finger, pointing it at him. Then she shouted.

"WEREWOLF!"

CHAPTER 11

Fuck.

Weylin winced as the sound of her shout did some serious damage to his supernaturally enhanced eardrums. He shook his head, waiting for her to continue with her freakout. Hell. She'd earned it.

But, to his surprise, Gwendolyn's face went from scared to pissed. She slapped his chest, turning on a dime with her hands on her hips and began talking so fast he could hardly catch up.

"You jerk! Here, I thought you were just some he-slut, trying to get into my pants and I was working damn hard to keep you firmly friend-zoned, but really, you were just trying to keep me from learning about this supernatural secret? I am such an idiot!"

"I was forbidden to tell you by my Alpha. He gave a command! Never mind the fact the Shifter Council would have my head if I told a human we existed without claiming her. But, I mean, if it helps, I do want to get into your pants," he mumbled, utterly confused.

"What? Hang on, we will circle back to that," she said, blinking slowly.

Her brown eyes seemed to darken at his words, and the Wolf in him rumbled appreciatively. Damn, she really was a knockout. Sassy as all hell, too, but he found that just as attractive.

"So, what you are saying is Werewolves exist?" she asked, moving away from him.

One minute he had his arms full of wiggling, sexy, curvy woman. The next they were cold and empty, and she was pointing and screaming names at him. Now, she was asking him questions when all he wanted to do was kiss her stupid.

"No. Yes. Sort of. We don't really call ourselves that," Weylin tried miserably to explain.

"Dude, what did you do to her?" Cole Mingan, his Pack mate, asked from the doorway.

The others had left, but this fuckhead had come running the second he heard Gwen's scream. Now the ponytail wearing asshat wouldn't leave. He'd been growing his hair out, and right then Weylin hated it.

"Why don't you get out of here? I got this," Weylin grunted.

"He can stay, maybe he can answer some stuff too," Gwen replied.

Well, damn. That was not what Weylin wanted at all. The thought dawned on him that maybe she was afraid of him. Like his Wolf would ever hurt her! Hell no. The monster inside him was loyal to her now. She had him, she did, mind, body, heart, and soul. He would do terrible things to make sure this woman felt safe and sound.

Hmm. Come to think of it, maybe she was right to fear him. He was a monster, and apparently, he had no scruples when it came to her. What kind of man would put one woman's needs above all others?

Him. He would. Gwen above all else. Always.

Grrrr.

"I think you better start from the beginning," Gwen said, head high, even if he could hear her heart hammering inside her chest.

"Okay. Well, the world is bigger than you think. Everything is not all black and white, Gwendolyn."

"I know all about religion and the soul. I was raised by a deacon, remember?"

"Yeah, but you see, that's the human world, the human soul, Gwen. I live in the supernatural world."

"The supernatural world?"

"Weylin! The fuck, man?" Cole hissed.

"Shut up, Cole. She is my mate. She has to hear the truth from me. I never should have tried to hide it! For days, man, I have watched on the fringes, waiting for the ideal time to try to talk to this woman, and it has been eating me alive."

"Shut up, man," Cole warned, grabbing him by the collar, but Weylin grabbed him right back.

"Do you know what happens to a Wolf who doesn't claim his fated mate? He loses his fucking mind, Cole. I can't take not knowing. Gwen deserves to know what she is to me, and I deserve to know if I have a shot at this," Weylin snarled, rejecting everything Derrick and all the rest of them had told him from the beginning.

"Stop! Wait! Is this all true?" Gwen asked, interrupting the two snarling Wolves.

Cole was still in Weylin's face, and he was growling at him. The bastard was at the same dominance level as him, and if he didn't back off, they were bound to scuffle.

Stop. Dangerous.

"You can't tell her about us man!"

"She's already seen, Cole! It's not a fucking secret anymore. Now, let's take it outside or you need to walk the fuck away," he grunted.

Weylin's Wolf was pissed off. Here was this asshole, grabbing onto his t-shirt collar and starting all kinds of shit just inches away from Weylin's mate. He could smell her anxiety and emotions, and it was making him even madder. He wrapped both hands around Cole's wrists and shoved the man away.

"Weylin, think man," Cole growled.

"I am thinking."

"You are threatening to out us all over some human, man—"

That was as far as Cole got. Weylin had enough of that fucking word, he punched his friend right in the jaw, just as the sound of glass smashing and the scent of whiskey filling the air.

"Stop it! Both of you!"

What the fuck? Weylin and Cole both turned to see petite and curvy Gwen waving a broken bottle at the two of them. Eyebrows raised, the two males separated, hands in the air. Shit. He didn't mean to scare her, but his Wolf was out of sorts, and Cole was pushing him too far.

"Whoa! Easy now, baby, why don't you set that

down on the desk, so no one gets hurt," Weylin suggested.

"Call me crazy, but I feel better with it in my hand. Now, excuse me for being *some human*, but someone better tell me what the fuck is going on!" Gwendolyn shouted.

"Language," Cole growled.

Weylin went to elbow him in the stomach, but the fucker dodged it. This was not at all how he'd imagined telling his mate about all this, but it looked like he had no choice.

"Cole, get the fuck out of here! Me and my mate need to talk."

"But I think—"

"Stop thinking and go," he growled.

"Weylin. Explain. Now." Gwendolyn's chest was heaving, but she was lowering her hand. That was progress.

"Shifters, that is what we are called, not Were-wolves, exist, Gwen. I am one," he said, eyeing the broken glass in her hand.

Her shoulders slumped as she absorbed his words, and with a shrug she threw the thing on the floor. Thank fuck. he was worried she would hurt herself.

"Okay. So, you are a Wolf Shifter?"

"Dire Wolf Shifter, actually. Our beasts are bigger, more powerful, older," he murmured, carefully observing her as he spoke.

"So, Shifters exist. Dire Wolf Shifters. Are you alone? Are there others?"

"Like me? Derrick, of course, he is our Alpha. Sheila, Cole, Thor, and Phoenix."

"Not Lucy?"

"Lucy is a Shifter, but not a Dire Wolf. She can tell you about that someday, maybe," he explained.

Gwen just nodded. He had to hand it to her. She was taking this all really well. Any other woman might have broken down, needed a drink, a pill, a week's paid vacation—but not Gwen. She just asked her questions and listened to his replies.

Not demanding. No hysterics. Yeah, she smashed a bottle, but he had a feeling that was more because he and Cole were seconds away from brawling at the time. Not now. Now she was almost eerily calm.

"So, there are other kinds of Shifters?"

"Yes. Shifters, supes, heck, there are many creatures in this world, Gwendolyn. Many levels of reality in the universe, or multiverse, even."

"Okay, hang on, I don't know if I can take all that right now," she said, biting her lip. "Ugh. It stinks in here like whiskey. I made such a mess," she mumbled.

"Don't worry about it. Someone will clean it. Did you want me to take you somewhere?"

"Home. Take me home, I need to think."

"Alright," he murmured, walking carefully behind her to his big SUV.

Worry gnawed at him. She seemed to be in a state of shock, all docile and quiet, which was hardly her norm. The drive to the motel took minutes, but Gwendolyn didn't speak during that time. She just looked out the window, her brown eyes clear but withdrawn.

Weylin cut the engine, pleased to see the usual group of shady characters were nowhere to be seen. Gwen remained seated, her eyes on the small concrete patio outside her front door.

"You've been here, haven't you? At night," she said.

"Yeah."

There was no point lying now. Fuck, his heart was breaking. Was this it? Would she say goodbye to him forever before he even got to know her?

"The, uh, manager told me my dog had to go. I was confused, but now it makes sense. He meant you," she said, turning to face him.

Weylin nodded, words failed him. The moon was almost full, its light shining in from the passenger window seemed to cast her in an ethereal glow. His mouth went dry, body straining, heart pumping as he stared helplessly at her.

He had never seen such raw, unspoiled beauty in a woman. So pure and with so much unrealized potential. Gwendolyn held all the cards here. She could end him with her rejection. Did she know that? He wondered, but kept the words to himself.

"Why? You never said why," she whispered.

"Why what?"

"Why me?"

"A million reasons, Gwen. The Fates paired us, for one thing. But more than that. I've been watching you since that first day and I've never seen anything like you," he murmured.

"You mean, you've never seen an old maid like me," she said with a self-deprecating snort.

"You choosing to wait is nothing to scoff at, baby. It means something, the value you placed on your-self. Your body is yours to share with who you choose when you're ready. I admire you so much for your choice, Gwen, I mean that," he told her, sincerity ringing in his words.

If only she could hear the truth as he spoke, he

mused. Bodies were cheap these days, but not Gwen. She knew her value, and he wanted to honor her for it. What a woman to stand against the current of what was popular and trending. She was an enigma. A wonder. A marvel.

Mine.

Not yet.

Hell, if he was ever lucky enough to have Gwendolyn choose him, he wanted it to be on her terms. Not his. He wanted her to pick him of her own free will. That would really be something.

Earning her love and trust? Fuck yeah.

That would be everything.

CHAPTER 12

Shifters existed. Dire Wolf Shifters, to be exact. Weylin Scott, the sexy, hot man who'd kissed her twice now, was one of them.

Holy. Crap.

She sat in his SUV outside the shitty motel she'd been living in, and she knew she should get out, leave him in peace. But she couldn't. Her body just wouldn't listen, and her mind had so many more questions.

"I, uh, that is, you probably have to go," she mumbled.

"I don't have to do anything, Gwendolyn. What's on your mind?" he whispered, careful to keep himself small, she realized.

Oh, he was good. Aware of her emotions, it

seemed, and tender with his actions. Weylin Scott was a mystery to her before she knew his big secret, and now, well, now he was a total enigma.

Why would a big, powerful man like that be interested in a curvy little nobody like her? Only one way to find out. Turning herself to face him, Gwendolyn straightened her shoulders, drawing in a deep breath.

"Why me?"

"Why you what?" he asked, green eyes wide.

"The kiss, well, both of them. The keeping guard at this shithole motel. You look like a man who has his pick of women, so why me? Is it because of what I said about saving myself for marriage? Am I just a challenge to you?"

"Hold on," he said, exhaling slowly. "First off, why not you? You're gorgeous, Gwen, and that's just a casual observation. Second, even if I could have anyone I want, I only want you. We have a legend," he began.

Gwen really started listening now. She was not going to be sidetracked by those emerald eyes, or his multifaceted hair, the muscles straining beneath his clothes, and his incredibly soft, exceptionally skilled pink lips. God, she could get lost in those lips.

His kisses were consuming. They were the kind

of thing she'd read about but never expected to find in real life. It was like all his attention was on her when he pressed his mouth to hers, and her promise to remain chaste until marriage abiding, Gwen was dying to indulge again.

What would it be like if she let go of that vow she made? If she gave herself to a man, no, *a Shifter*, like him? She'd had her heart broken before, and sex had had nothing and yet everything to do with it.

Would Weylin break her heart? Even if he did, she'd bet the farm he would make it worth her while. There was something so primal about her need for him. Gwen could not help her reactions to the man. The way he looked, the way he smelled, the way he moved—everything drew her to him like some invisible magnet.

Wait. Was he talking? What was he saying?

"I said, we have a legend," he murmured, a hint of a grin playing at the corner of his mouth. "That is, *supernaturals* have a legend."

"About what?" she asked, curious about legends that had their own legends.

"About fated mates," he said, his voice so deep and rumbly it sent chills traveling up her spine.

"Fated mates. What's that?"

"A fated mate is like a soul mate. It's the one

person or persons the Fates created just for you. The soul that can make yours complete. Fated mates are everything to each other."

"Wow. That's a fantastic notion," she said.

"Yeah. It is. A lot of folks believe it is pure fantasy, and it gets confusing, and lines get muddled. People think having a fated mate means you have no choice, but that isn't true. And it isn't just a supernatural thing, humans have fated mates as well. Supes are just better able to spot them, is all."

"So, are you saying I have a fated mate?"

"Yeah, you do, Gwen," he whispered, eyes glowing in the darkness of the vehicle.

"What about you? Do you have a fated mate, Weylin?"

"Yes," he hissed the word.

The air seemed electrified, with whatever aware-ness was sizzling between them. Her skin burned, seeming to want his touch. Gwen swayed slightly towards him. She was so close, tiny specks of gold glittered in his green gaze, dazzling her with their depths.

"My Dire Wolf knew the second I spotted you. You were always meant to be mine, Gwendolyn Hoffer."

"How can you be sure?" she whispered, scared to

raise her voice lest it break the spell weaving between them.

"Oh, I'm sure. It was like the whole world had been slightly askew my entire life, then you came into it, and everything was right, for the first time ever. The Fates set you right in my path, and I am so fucking grateful. You make everything right, Gwen."

"But where's the choice in that?" she murmured, swallowing softly.

"It's not enough for me to see you and know what you are to me. You have to want me, too."

"I see," she replied softly.

Their heads were so close now, one small move and she'd be touching him, kissing him. God, she wanted to. How she wanted to! But what would it mean, giving her heart to a monster? Listening to her gut instincts about him, she suddenly knew this was right. Weylin Scott was different from the rest. He was special.

Safe. Tender. Caring. Real.

"Yes or no, Gwen. I have to know if you want this, baby. Tell me, please," he whispered, his plea tender, endearing.

The soft, warm tickle of his breath had her trembling in the passenger seat. Gwen inhaled the woodsy scent she'd come to associate with the giant redhead, and she felt her insides warm with recognition.

"I trusted a boy with my heart once," she began.

Weylin cocked his head. He listened to her, and that was a marvel in and of itself. She felt his confusion, but his patience outweighed it, or overruled it, and that was one of the things she was starting to love about him. It was way too soon for that word, she thought, and winced, but went on with what she had to say.

"He betrayed me. He just wanted someone to warm his bed, and when I wouldn't, when I told him I had made a vow to save myself for marriage, he found someone else who didn't have the same hangups as me."

"I'm sorry," he replied, brows furrowed.

"After, he told me I wasn't worth the wait. He said nobody would want to wait for a frigid little fat girl and I'd better think twice before life passed me by."

"Where does he live now?"

"Oh stop," she laughed. "I don't need you to avenge me, Weylin. What I want to know is what do you think?"

"About you? I know for you it's been a few days, but for me, it's been decades. But Gwen, you are worth the wait. My fated mate, Gwen, that is what you are. I'd spend forever waiting if I knew you were going to be there in the end."

"You would?" she asked, and when he nodded, something inside her just clicked.

Gwendolyn believed him. It was like her heart had taken a leap of faith, and now it was pounding like a herd of buffalo through the plains. Holy crap. Could she die of this?

"No. I wouldn't let anything hurt you, baby. Not ever," he whispered just before she crushed her mouth to his.

Fireworks exploded as their lips melded to each other. And oooh, but he was even better at this than she'd thought. There went the earth, just like he described it, spinning out of orbit, then righting itself again.

He was a patient teacher, cupping her face tenderly in his hands until she got used to the way their mouths fit. He reached back with one hand, holding onto her neck, moving her just so. Then his tongue was sliding past hers in a dance old as time.

She reached out with shaky hands to steady herself, clutching his wide shoulders, which was damn hard to do in the confines of the car. The center console was in the way, but Weylin pushed on something, a button maybe, then slid the thing back, and pulled her flush against him.

She felt the power he kept so tightly contained, and it moved her almost as much as his skilled lips and tongue. Oh God, she had no idea what she was doing, but he was a good leader. He cradled her head with one hand, holding her there, while the other threaded in her hair as he worked his tongue in and out against hers.

He tasted good, she thought as she swallowed him down. Licking and lapping at one another like they could not breathe without the other. Maybe they couldn't. Is that what fated mates meant?

Her body heated, nipples hardened, and that place between her legs ached with a need she had never felt. It was like fantasy and biology were taking over her mind, some magical combination of the two and they were causing her to soak her panties. Or maybe that was just him.

Gwen thought she knew how to kiss, but this was a whole other level of lip locking. Weylin was a god here and for the first time, Gwen couldn't wait for what came next. She wanted, *no*, she needed more. She needed him.

"Gwen," he moaned, pressing his forehead to hers.

"Come inside with me," she moaned.

"I don't wanna rush you, baby. We can take our time," he growled, but she instinctively knew this was hurting him.

That was the last thing she wanted. Truth be told, ever since meeting him, that fateful night when she'd walked into the bar, Gwen hadn't been able to stop thinking about him. Weylin Scott had taken more of her time than she cared to admit. But maybe she could now that she knew what she was to him.

Mate. You are my mate.

"You're not rushing me. I told you I made a mistake before trusting a boy, I think maybe this time I try trusting a Wolf."

Mine.

CHAPTER 13

He almost fell getting out of the SUV, her smile was blinding and the hardness in his jeans was making it difficult to think. But the second he did manage to exit the vehicle, Weylin snarled.

The scent of urine and feces, filth and degradation surrounded them. He wanted to claim Gwendolyn as his own, but not there. Not in that awful place. He got back in the car and started the thing.

"What are you doing?" she asked, confused.

"Need you somewhere safe. Gwen. Need to take you to my den," he growled, more Wolf than man.

She nodded, but he could scent the shame coming from her. Fuck. He was being a dick, and that was the last thing he wanted. He stopped the car at a red light, grabbed her hand, and kissed her palm.

"I'm sorry I know that place—" she started.

"Don't you dare apologize. Brave, hardworking, loyal, humble woman. You steal my breath with your strength."

"I thought maybe you were ashamed," she whispered, and he heard her gasp, the soft sound breaking his heart.

"Ashamed of you? Never. My beast won't let me claim you inside that place. Monster that he is, my Wolf wants me to burn it to the fucking ground. You're so good, Gwen. So worthy, love, can't you see? My animal would have me rope the moon for you if you said so," he murmured, wiping her tears.

She laughed then and kissed his palm, and fuck, it was like lightning striking through his body. Already he felt his bond to her growing. Amazing, since they'd only ever kissed.

Oh, but she was magic, this sassy, curvy human with her warm eyes, and curly hair. Pure magic, and it thrilled him to the marrow that she was saying yes. That she trusted him with her most precious gift —*herself.*

He drove back in the direction of the bar, past the Pack house, to where he'd built a small cottage for himself. It was just five rooms—*bedroom, bathroom, kitchen, living room, and a small closed-in porch*—but he had plans to increase that should he ever find himself in need of more space.

"This is perfect," she said, and he heard the smile in her voice before he turned to see it.

"Wait there."

The almost full moon was low in the sky as he ran around the car to open the door. She grinned shyly as he scooped her up in his arms, loving the weight of her. Slight thing she was and always concerned about her size. Weylin shook his head. She was perfect for him, and he was going to spend every day loving on her until she believed him. Even then, he had no plans to ever stop.

Gwendolyn laced her arms around his neck, resting her cheek against his. Fuck, his breath caught in his throat as her strawberry scent grew sweet with her arousal. The woman had him hotter than a firecracker, and he was bound to go off any second if she didn't stop pressing those sweet little kisses to his throat.

Don't ever stop.

He walked straight through to the bedroom, dropping her gently on the coverlet atop the king-sized mattress. Gwen squeaked, and he cursed himself for being an oaf.

"Sorry," he murmured, nerves causing him to freeze in place.

Where had all his prowess gone? Fuck. he was no green pup, and yet one look at his gorgeous, *and virginal,* mate sitting on his bed had Weylin at a complete fucking loss as to where to start.

"Come here," she murmured, using the crux of her finger to lure him closer.

How was she so cool? So calm? She was the virgin here. Not him. And yet.

"Kiss me," she whispered, cupping his cheeks, and Weylin loosed a soft growl as she pressed her mouth to his.

Virgin or not, there was no question who was in charge here, he thought, moaning as she slid her fingers beneath the hem of his shirt. Gwendolyn sat on the bed, legs splayed while he kneeled on the floor in front of her.

Fuck, she was tiny. Sweet, petite, and so damn hot. His growl was almost constant now as she lifted his shirt, with him helping to remove the confounded thing from his too hot skin. Goose-bumps broke out across his sin as she ran her nails up and down his abdomen, chest, and shoulders.

"Gwen, my Gwen," he whispered, licking intently at her lips, chin, and neck.

He cupped her breast territorially, claiming the soft flesh as his, swallowing her moan when she pressed against him. Thunder roared between his ears, and he pressed his covered cock against the apex of her thighs. Fuck, he couldn't get close enough. He was on fire for her. Body aching, pulse racing, heart hammering, when he opened his eyes from this last kiss to see Gwen's own molten chocolate gaze boring into his, he knew she was more than ready.

"Mine," he growled, gripping her shirt and waiting for her brisk nod to proceed.

He undressed her slowly, like the gift she was. Kissing every inch of flesh revealed, Weylin memorized every freckle and beauty mark, every touch that brought with it a whimper or sigh. He tried to go slow, really, he tried, but Gwendolyn was more passionate than he could have ever dreamed she would be.

"You drive me wild, baby," he murmured, leaning over her on top of the mattress.

Their kissing and heavy petting had raised the temperature in the cabin, so hot it might as well have been a sauna. Not that he minded. The woman conjured fires inside him to the depths of his soul, and he was more than willing to follow her into the flames.

"Oh, Weylin," she moaned his name, sending shivers through his body at the hushed sound.

She was magic, this woman. Pure, unadulterated magic, and every cell in his body was attuned to her pleasure.

Weylin captured her nipple between his lips, kissing and sucking the bud until it hardened for him. Strawberries and cream, he thought with a growl as he licked a trail from one breast to the other, coveting her, worshipping her like the goddess she was.

His cock thumped against his briefs, hard as steel and begging for release, but he couldn't go to her like this. Like some rutting animal, even if it was half true. She was virginal and untried, and the last thing he wanted was to scare her or, gods forbid, hurt her in any way. But like everything else about her, Gwendolyn was surprisingly forward in her carnal desires.

She clutched at his shoulders when he slid down her body, kissing her breasts, belly and thighs as he did. He loved how soft she was, how smooth her skin felt. The short crop of curls that topped her sex were dark and silky, he parted her slick folds with his fingers, keeping her gaze on his as he placed a kiss on her nether lips.

"You can't—oh, yes, you can," she moaned as he kissed and suckled on her womanly flesh, nibbling her pink bits until she writhed mindlessly beneath his ministrations.

He sounded positively feral as he ate her sweet pussy. His growl built and built, reverberating in the bedroom as he licked and sucked, adding one than two fingers as he worked and stretched her, readying her for his possession.

Gwendolyn cried out, pulling his hair as her first orgasm took over. He moved quickly then, sliding up her heated body, positioning himself at her entrance, and pressing home as she came harder with the first flex of his steely cock into her core.

"Weylin!" she cried out, and he snarled and held still.

Fuck. She was tight. Tight. Hot. And his.

"Mine," he growled, heated stare capturing hers, holding it as he started to move.

"Yours," she replied, nodding even as she welcomed him with a desperate whimper.

Fuck. She was new to this. He had to remember that. It was easy once his animal understood, and he coveted her so. Beautiful, brave, strong woman.

Slick, sexy, wet heat surrounded him, and Weylin lost himself in loving her.

My woman. My mate. My everything.

Rearing up on his knees. He pulled her body with him, wrapping her legs around his waist. Weylin crashed his mouth to hers, lifting her up and down on his cock until she was gasping with another, stronger climax.

"Weylin!" She gasped, eyes wide with shock and awe as he took her even higher.

Now! The time was now. His beast demanded it. He had to claim his fated mate right then and there. She wanted commitment, well what he was giving her was more than even she might have bargained for.

"Gwendolyn, I claim you here now, mine, mate," he growled, his body moving urgently now.

"Yes. Oh, yes!"

And that was all the permission he needed. Weylin slammed Gwen down on his cock, lifted her hair off her shoulder, and sunk his teeth into her flesh, marking her with his bite and claiming her as his own for now and all time.

"Mine!" he roared as seed spurted from his cock, coating her walls, and filling her with his scent.

———

Weylin cradled Gwen in his arms, cuddling her closely as they both tried to catch their breaths. Thirty years she'd held onto her virginity, only to give it away to a, *well, make that to her,* Wolf man.

Did she have any regrets? None. Weylin was everything she could have ever wanted in a lover and more. So much more.

"Are you alright?" he asked, his growly voice kindling something in her belly.

She turned to face him, loving the way he could not seem to stop touching her. He was really so handsome, she mused, tracing a line from his thick, silky red locks, down to his copper eyebrows and lashes, past his straight nose, and stubborn chin. Smiling, she leaned into him, kissing his lips, loving the way he seemed so ready with a kiss just for her.

"Does it hurt?" he asked, and for a moment, she wondered what he meant.

"I feel good, actually, not sore like the books said," she replied, then realized he was looking at her shoulder.

Oh yeah. He bit her.

"Why did you bite me?" she asked, as she looked

down at the already healed puncture wounds his teeth made.

"Sorry I didn't tell you first, baby," he murmured, kissing her booboo, and then pressing his forehead to hers. "It is part of the claiming ritual. I thought I could wait till, well, that is to say, until the next time we, er—"

"Made love? Had sex? Did the dirty? Boinked? Fucked like bunnies?"

"Gwen!" he said, shocked. He was laughing as he tickled her mercilessly for her description of what they did. Truth was, it went beyond words for her. Even as she landed on top of him, heat began to stir in her nether regions, and she opened her legs just to feel his rigid length against her core.

"Gwen, I want you so badly," he murmured, but for some dang reason, he was holding back.

"Want you too, please," she moaned, finding him with her hands.

"Don't wanna hurt you, baby," he confessed.

So that was why? Well, she might not know a lot about this, but she wanted to know more, With him. Maybe Gwen was just lucky or something because there was no pain, only pleasure. She placed his head at her entrance, thrilling at the size and hardness of him as she slid down, taking him deep, so deep inside.

"What do you want? Anything, anything at all, I will give it to you," Weylin growled, fingers digging into her hips.

"I only want the truth from you."

"You have it, Gwen. I swear."

"Good. And you have me, always," she replied, then she started moving.

CHAPTER 14

Waking up with his mate in his arms, in a tangle of sheets, with the sunlight streaming in through the blinds, was definitely up there on Weylin's top three things to do of all time. First, was kissing her. Second, was making love to her.

Hmm.

Maybe there should be a fourth thing too. Like when she smiled. Fuck yeah. Weylin loved it when she smiled.

"Morning, baby," he grinned when she stirred.

"Good morning," she replied, her cheeks pink with exertion, sleep, or perhaps a tendril left of shyness.

Though, after everything they'd done during the

night, he would be hard pressed to ponder that one. He'd kissed, touched, and loved on every inch of his delectable little mate. And she'd done the same to his delight and her unending curiosity.

Leaning down, Weylin slipped his hands beneath the sheet covering her hip and traced her curves. She gazed up at him with lusty, soulful eyes that stole his breath. Sexy woman, looking so well-loved and perfect in his arms, in his bed, in his life. He kissed her quick, wanting to make her breakfast since he'd heard her stomach growling almost an hour ago. But she was so warm and comfy, he didn't want to jostle her until she woke up herself.

"How's a dozen pancakes sound to you?" he asked, loving the way her eyes sparkled as she bit her bottom lip and nodded.

"Sounds amazing. Got any blueberries and lemons?"

"Yeah. Why?" he asked curiously.

"Cause we are gonna add some lemon zest and a cup of blueberries to the batter and you are gonna love it."

"Oh, I am, am I?"

"Yep."

Forty-minutes, and some tussling on the bath-room floor later, and Gwendolyn was sitting down at his kitchen counter beside him, a stack of blue-berry lemon pancakes between them. She giggled and fed him the first bite, which Weylin took too fast, almost dying in the process. Fucking things were hot.

"Oh my God, you should see your face right now!" Gwen chuckled. "You are breathing smoke like a dragon."

"I'm a Dire Wolf, baby. We are way cooler than Dragons."

"Wait, those are real?" she asked, eyes wide.

"Gwendolyn, how many times do I have to tell you the multiverse is a big place filled with wonders," he said, feeding her a normal-sized bite.

She made a little chomping sound as she chewed, and fuck, it was cute. He grinned, watching her, falling for her more with every passing second.

"So, we're mated now, right?"

"Yep."

"And no weird side effects, right? Shifters aren't like Werewolves in the movies," she said, and Weylin's heart started pounding.

"Um, well, far as I know. It has been a long time since a Dire Wolf mated a human," he murmured.

"So, I might get a tail?" she asked, stunned.

"Nah. Um, I mean, I don't think so," he mumbled,

making a mental note to talk to Derrick. "Hey, I promise, anything happens to you, and I will be right here, okay?"

"Okay, yeah," she murmured and sat up straighter.

It was Sunday, but they were going to visit her Pop after breakfast. Weylin had a little surprise, he hoped she wouldn't mind.

He was nervous about the awkward conversation they'd had at breakfast, but after a while, she seemed to relax. The drive went by quickly, and soon they were headed inside Hope Springs.

"Where's Pop?" Gwendolyn gasped, walking right to the old room her grandfather had shared with another patient.

"I hope it's alright since we're mates now," he told her, placing his hands on her shoulders and turning her around. "I had his package upgraded. I know you want him to have the best care, Gwen, and it is the least I can do for the man who raised my mate."

Weylin paused, trying to gauge her reaction. She was looking over his shoulder, her big brown eyes glassy with unshed tears. His stomach turned in knots and he rubbed the back of his head.

"Gwen, fuck, I am so sorry, I should have asked

—" he started, but she jumped on him, hugging him so tight he could hardly breathe.

"Thank you," she whispered, and he felt warm tears seep into his shirt where her face was pressed against his shoulder.

"It's alright. Shhh, hey, come on. Let's go see him," he said, cupping her pretty, heart-shaped face in his hands and dropping a kiss on her lips.

It was too soon, but his heart glowed with love for her. Love? No. Yes, his Wolf pushed. Stupid, red-furred monster was preening with it. Fuck. The realization dawned so suddenly, Weylin tripped on his way down the hall.

"You okay?" she asked, turning her head to check on him as they followed the directions on the map to the private suites.

"Yep. Fine," he replied, but was he?

Mating was one thing, but falling in love was something else entirely. Some folks were built for love, he knew. Like Derrick and Lucy, even though the Alpha fem had been reluctant at first. Kind of like Sheila and Leo, who rejected the Lion before she finally accepted his claim. Their relationship sure was weird.

Brock and Ariella were a loving couple, though he'd had some psychological issues to get past before they got together. And Tracey and Phoenix, though she had some personal shit too, from what Phoenix said.

Maybe love wasn't for people who were perfect. Maybe it was just for couples who were willing to give it their all. Folks who knew the value of their partner and wanted to honor and keep them safe and happy. That was all he wanted, and he was more than willing to work hard for it.

Watching Gwen walk down the hall in her jeggings and white crop top made Weylin realize it didn't matter if he thought he was worthy or not. He was already in love with the woman.

She was the keeper of his heart. The other half to his soul. She had the fealty of his beast. And he would live every day just to see her smile. Oh yes, loving Gwendolyn was easy as breathing, and even more rewarding. It was necessary. Vital. And he would not have it any other way.

"You coming?" she asked, excitement in her voice as she waited outside the door to Pop's new room.

Mine.

"Yes."

Weylin joined her inside the spacious suite, standing back while she greeted her grandfather. The older man seemed to be having a good day as recognition sparkled in his warm chocolate eyes. So like Gwen's, Weylin thought as he shook the man's hand.

"I see my Gwennie has a fella. You do right by her, boy, or I'll come looking for you," Pop warned, only half-teasing.

"Don't worry, sir. I promise to take care of her."

"You guys, I am standing right here," she complained, but her eyes were glossy and her smile wide as she held Pop's hand with one of hers, and Weylin's in the other.

"You did good, Gwennie," Pop said, and prided filled Weylin as he watched her give her grandfather a kiss on the cheek.

They would not have the old man forever, but with his mood improved, and Weylin's new connection to his mate, he could see the familial bonds tying the old man to Gwendolyn. Without knowing if it would work, he tried pushing a little light into that bond, hoping for the best.

They stayed there, playing cards, and later, Gwen read aloud to Pop from one of her infamous romance novels. Weylin had to remember to ask to borrow that one, since she skipped the steamy scenes. The three of them remained together until a nurse shooed them away with a report from the doctor that Pop's health was improving, and he was quite comfortable in his new room.

It was early evening by the time they got back home, and Weylin growled contentedly as he lifted Gwen from the passenger seat. Sweetheart that she was, she'd worn herself out making sure her grandfather had enough of his favorite foods and easy access to the TV remote and nurses' call button. She'd dozed off almost as soon as she got into his car.

"Mmm. Are we home?" she asked.

"Yeah, baby. Hey, do you feel okay?" Weylin asked, suddenly on alert.

Her skin was on fire, and his wolf had perked up almost immediately upon touching her. A cool, fall breeze rustled the leaves near his cabin, but Weylin took no time to enjoy the scenery. Something was wrong here.

"Derrick!" he shouted, knowing full well the Alpha would hear him across the patch of grass that sat between the Pack house and his cabin.

He hustled inside, placing her down on the sofa. Weylin started by removing her jacket, shoes, and socks. He ran a clean washcloth under the faucet and came back with it in his hands, pressing it to her head. Gwen moaned, curling up on the couch with her hands across her stomach.

"What's happened?" Derrick asked as he pushed his way inside without knocking.

"I don't know. She's sick or something. My Wolf is freaking out," Weylin growled, kneeling down on the hardwood floor beside Gwen.

"Hey," Lucy said, hands on her belly as she walked over to them and felt Gwendolyn's head. "She has a fever."

Weylin growled helplessly as Lucy doctored his mate. Worry consumed him, and the beast inside was raging.

"Did you claim her?" Derrick asked sternly. His eyes glowed with his Wolf as he followed Weylin's nod.

"Yes. But I'm not sick, Alpha. Fuck, we don't get sick! Are humans allergic to the bite?"

"You bit her? Even though she's human?"

Weylin nodded, swallowing down the bile threatening to out itself from his lips. Fear clenched his stomach, and his Dire Wolf was shredding him from the inside out. After everything, he'd finally claimed his mate, and what—he made her sick?

Shit. No. This couldn't be happening.

Please, please be okay.

"I'm calling Thor. He might know something," Derrick grumbled, pulling his cell phone from his pocket.

Weylin nodded, sweat dotting his brow. Gwendolyn moaned loud. Lucy was still holding her hand, her big blue eyes darted from Gwen's prone body to Weylin's drawn face.

"She feels so hot, Wey. I don't know what this could be," the Alpha fem said, looking concerned.

The pounding of footsteps reached the cabin, and Weylin moved in front of Gwen. He couldn't help it. His Wolf was going nuts.

"Easy," Derrick commanded, using his Alpha voice. But something freaky was happening.

Weylin growled at his Alpha, lowering his gaze, but snarling, nonetheless.

"You bit her when? Last night? During a full moon?" Thor asked, entering the house.

"It wasn't full yet," Weylin growled.

"Close enough, brother," Thor replied, his eyes glittering like black onyx as he moved towards Gwen.

Weylin snapped his teeth, grabbing his Pack mate's beefy arm as he tried to pass. He could not help it. The Wolf was out of his mind with protective instincts, and Pack mate or not, he did not want anyone near Gwen save for the Alpha fem.

"I must assess her, brother Wolf. I will not harm your mate. I swear it," Thor told him in a voice deep with his animal.

Thor was perhaps the quietest Wolf among them. Weylin trusted the man with his life but asking him to trust him with his mate's life. Well, that was something else.

Something pushed its way through the Pack bonds, his intentions, Weylin realized, and his Wolf rumbled approvingly. The Dire Wolf MC was more than a Pack, it was a family. They had built their bonds on friendship, trust, and affection.

"Sex, blood, a full moon, and your sacred vow to love this woman have all converged to make the impossible happen, my brother," Thor said in a rumbly voice.

Thor looked at Weylin, just as Gwen's back arched and she roared a loud, horrible sound full of pain that tore at his heart. Thor growled, then he gripped the waistband of Gwen's pants. Fury hit him hard, but before Weylin could move, Derrick and Cole were tackling him as Thor tore the clothes off his mate's body a single moment before a wave of power knocked them all on their asses.

Next, the impossible happened. A dark brown Wolf ripped out of his mate, and she was ferocious. The animal lunged for Cole, nipping him on the ass and forcing the idiot to let go of Weylin. Derrick did not have to worry about that. The Alpha was smarter than he looked, releasing the male who was already on his knees and reaching for his incredible mate.

"Gwendolyn?" he asked, wonder lacing his raspy voice as the huge she-Wolf butted heads with him.

I thought you said no secrets, Weylin.

"I didn't know, baby, I swear," he said, smiling through tears of wonder as he ran his hands over her fur. "*Ohmyfuck!* Are you talking in my head?"

I think so. Weylin, come with me. Let's run.

Gwendolyn yipped, making a circle in the living room, and knocking Cole over in the process. The butthead had only just found his feet. Oh, well. He had it coming, Weylin was sure.

"I think your mate wants to run with you, brother," Thor said, a smile on his usually somber face.

CHAPTER 15

The entire world had changed, or maybe it was just Gwen.

She raced through the Blue Valley forest with her new eyes keenly taking stock of the land. Her mate was hot on her heels, but this new body was fast and strong. She vaulted over a creek, landing in a pile of freshly fallen autumn leaves with a happy bark.

She'd gone from alone to mated to the most handsome man she had ever seen, with a beast of a Wolf inside her in less than a week, but if you asked her if she had any regrets. Gwendolyn would have to say no. It was only the truth.

For what seemed like hours, she and Weylin ran and walked through the forest together. When her fur started to tingle and her muscles twitched, she turned scared eyes to her mate, whose own emerald gaze was calm and knowing.

It's okay. You just have to change back, he said, speaking through their matebond.

She had learned so much that night. Things she had never dreamed of back in her Sunday school classes, or even in college in Manhattan. The world was a lot bigger than she knew, but instead of feeling scared and lost, Gwen felt good. IN fact, she felt better about it than ever before.

There were infinitesimal mysteries out there, but she belonged right here. With Weylin, with the Pack, with her Pop for however long she had him, and that was all she really needed.

How do I change back?

Just picture your human self, Gwen. Hold on to that image in your mind's eye and let the magic wash over you.

I can't! I, but before panic set in, Weylin was there in his skin, on his knees before her.

"It's okay, baby. Just picture her. You got this. I'm here," he murmured encouragingly, and Gwendolyn allowed her trust in him to fill her.

Lord, it was amazing having someone believe in her besides her grandfather. The way Weylin looked at her, a mixture of pride, love, and possession, warmed her to her marrow. Heated her insides, made her body tingle with anticipation.

She did as he said, held onto the image of her in her human skin. Just Gwendolyn. With him. Her mate. Her bones began to snap, muscle tearing, reknitting itself into her other shape. It took a few minutes, and she knew it wasn't pretty, but he stayed right where he was.

Good mate, that new inner voice, her she-Wolf, growled in a huskier version of Gwendolyn's voice.

Yes, she had to agree. He was good, and he was her mate. Earnest green eyes glittered down at her, hands hovering but not touching, as Weylin waited for every last tingle and ache to fade from her shivering skin. But Gwen wasn't as patient as him.

The second she could move on her own, she was reaching for him, crawling into his lap as she placed a thousand kisses on his skin and sighed against him. Love like she never even knew was possible filled her to the brim.

"Was this how you felt all along? Was it just like this?" she asked, eyes wide with wonder as she cupped his face and kissed him with everything she had.

"Yes, and no. I'm not as brave as you, fierce, bold, sassy thing that you are, my Gwendolyn. I was afraid to even think the word I can hear from you. Fuck, it's filling my head, and it is so damn beautiful," he whispered, holding her face and kissing her hard. "Love you so much, Gwen. Love you, my mate. My fated for me and only me, mate," he growled.

"I love you, too, Weylin. So damn much I can't breathe without saying it. It's like nothing I ever felt," she whispered in awe of this wonderful man who'd given her so many incredible gifts.

"I will spend the rest of my life making sure you never feel even a moment's regret," he growled.

"Let's start now," she said, moving her hips against him, loving the way his body reacted so readily to hers.

Weylin's eyes glittered with his Wolf, and she felt hers rear up to meet him through her stare. Oh, she loved his beast, loved the man, too, and was desperate to show him. Gwendolyn was still new to the physical side of loving, but it was fun with him. He made it all seem easy as breathing.

"That's it, baby. Take me. Take all of me," he growled and positioned her over his ready cock.

Her head fell back, hair a hopeless tangle, but Gwendolyn was beyond caring as he filled her with his hardened length. The man really was a god, she mused as he lifted her and pulled her down again, filling her to the hilt until they were both panting, desperate with the need to come.

He was turning her into lava from the inside out. Creating wildfires with every touch and brush of his skin against hers. Gwendolyn gasped, digging her fingers into his wide shoulders and arching her back. Weylin roared a little then, flipping them over so that she was flat on the bed of moss he'd somehow found for them.

She mewled, needing him to move again, but he sat there, buried deep and staring at her, running his hands over her body from her neck, over her breasts and soft belly, to strum that tiny nubbin peeking through her curls. Gwen hissed, and he growled his reply, flexing his hips and sliding that deliciously long cock in and out, all the while flicking his thumb over her nubbin.

Pleasure danced along her skin, anticipation of what was to come, *mainly her*, sizzled up her spine. Yes, yes, yes. She loved what he was doing. Every sound of his body sliding out of hers. Every welcoming slap of skin against skin as he pushed back in. Each breath, grunt, groan, whimper, and sigh. She loved all of it. All of him.

"More, please," she begged, and her mate did not make her beg again.

Though, to be honest, Gwendolyn would not have minded. His dick was heavy and hard, wet with her pleasure as he pumped, pumped, pumped, bringing them higher and higher until she thought she would burst with it. She loved the feral expression on his face, the fierce glint in his eye as he grabbed her hip with one hand, stroking her clit faster with the other.

"Come for me, mate. Now," Weylin growled, more Wolf than man.

Gwen was already there. But with his command, her body broke apart. Flying into the sun, that was what it felt like. Her orgasm shot through her with all the heat and power of that enormous star, creating a gravity field all of its own, pulling Gwendolyn and Weylin right into orbit.

Weylin's body spasmed jerkily as he rode out his orgasm with her, dragging hers out in the process until she was too weak to move. He slumped over her, careful not to crush her with his tremendous size, though she would have welcomed his weight. Instead, he curled on his side and pulled her back, cuddling her close.

"Mine," he murmured, still trying to catch his breath as he kissed her shoulder and her neck, sniffing deeply where they met.

"So, do I smell weird now?" she asked, only now processing some of her newfound powers, which included one hell of a sniffer.

"Not weird. Good. You always smell good, Gwen. Like strawberries. But now you smell like me, too," Weylin told her.

She could hear the smile in his voice as he said, and something animalistic inside her approved of his possessive snarl. Gwen smiled contentedly, realizing she was a tad bit psycho, *er*, proprietorial herself. Her eyes grew heavy, and her breathing slowed as she found peace beside her mate. The steady beat of his heart soothed her nerves, and she dozed off in no time.

"Come on, baby. Let's get you home," he said, after what seemed like minutes.

Gwendolyn sat up, realizing she was off the ground already and in Weylin's strong arms. The evening had turned to full on night sometime after she had closed her eyes, and she yawned, glancing up at the full moon smiling down on them.

"Mm. I am pretty heavy, you know. You sure you got me, mate?" she asked, rubbing his shoulders and kissing his neck.

"I got you, Gwendolyn. Always," Weylin growled,

slapping a kiss across her lips and carrying her home.

Home. That sounded nice to her ears, and she smiled, knowing Weylin was her real home. The Fates had brought them together, and Gwendolyn had never felt so whole before. It was going to be some adjustment from what she was then and what she was now, but with Weylin, and the Pack, she was confident it would be okay.

"What's going on in that head of yours, love?" she asked Weylin, noting the Cheshire cat grin that seemed stuck on his face.

"I was just thinking, you know you have to marry me now, right?"

"What?"

"Yep. You were saving yourself for marriage, and you gave yourself to me, so you gotta marry me! Ha! We're gonna beat Derrick and Lucy to the altar," he said, seeming to find that amusing.

"What are you saying? Who says I'd even have you?" Gwen teased.

"What?"

"You didn't even propose, Weylin. Now who's to say some handsome man might not come along and get down on his knees and ask to marry me tomorrow?"

She looked over her shoulder at him, crossing the room as she opened the bathroom door. Poor man had his eyes glued to her ass, but they shot up when he realized what she said. Too bad she was already headed for the shower.

"What? Gwen? GWEN! Open that door, Gwendolyn," he growled, pounding on the thing.

She turned on the water and started humming over Weylin's shenanigans. Of course, she was going to marry him. But when she said, not the other way around.

Silly man, thinking he held the strings.

The shower curtain flew back, and Weylin stood there, chest heaving, eyes glittering, and finger raised at eye level.

"Gwendolyn Hoffer, you are my mate and I absolutely forbid you marrying anyone but me!"

"Is that so?" she asked, brows arched as he growled at her. "Then might I suggest you get down on your knees, mate?" she growled, bottom lip between her teeth, as he finally understood what she was suggesting.

"Yes, ma'am," he growled and slid to the floor, large hands wrapped around her thighs.

Weylin's green eyes danced with delight as he

lifted one, slinging it over his shoulder, and kissed her right on her needy little sex.

"Mine," he snarled, and Gwendolyn gripped his hair, nodding her head.

Yes, she was his. And tonight, she planned to claim him right back.

Mine.

EPILOGUE

"Honey, I am home!" Gwendolyn shouted as she entered the cabin she shared with her mate and her husband.

They really had been bad, running off to Atlantic City to get married over the weekend, but that was what they both wanted. It eased something inside her that had held onto her vow for all those years, even though her new Wolf side understood being mated was just as important as being married.

She spent the last couple of hours changing her name at the DMV, and the nearest Social Security office, and all she really wanted was to go for a run with her mate, then dinner, and some celebratory love making under the stars. Not necessarily in that order.

"Weylin?" she tried again, but he wasn't answering.

Gnawing her lip, she walked to the kitchen table, smiling when she saw a single red rose and folded letter written in his handwriting. The sexy scrawl made her heart flutter, and she sighed like a lovesick teenager when she opened it.

Dear Gwendolyn,

I have a surprise for you. It's good, I promise. Meet me at the Pack house.

Love always,

Weylin

Gwendolyn crushed the letter to her chest, smiling widely as she grabbed the rose too, dropped her keys and bag, and raced across the lot to the Pack house. Everyone was there, and she frowned, wondering if she missed a Pack meeting.

Something about how she came to be a Dire Wolf Shifter meant her bonds were more solid to Weylin than to anyone else. Still, she scented him among the others, and knew he was inside. But she wasn't prepared for the sight that met her eyes when she walked inside.

Weylin, sans shirt, was on his knees, head bowed. The entire Pack stood shoulder to shoulder in a circle around him. Only Thor was with him. The bald giant seemed different, as if he wasn't seeing anything through his impossibly black eyes. At least, nothing she could see.

"What's going on?" she asked, and Weylin's head snapped up, his emerald eyes boring into hers.

"Gwen," he breathed, and smiled.

"Weylin?" she said again, uncertainty cracking her voice.

Her inner beast wanted to tuck tail and run. There was magic there, ancient and powerful. Something strange was happening, strange and important, she realized, taking in the somber atmosphere.

Thor began chanting in a language she did not recognize. The enormous man moved quietly, taking what looked like sticks and a jar of something murky out of a box.

"Come," Lucy whispered, and the woman looked incredible considering her tummy dropped, and her pup was going to be born any day now.

"He's speaking in an old, forgotten tongue. Those markings are the ancient glyphs of the original Dire Wolf Pack, the first ones," she whispered, explaining what was happening even as Sheila placed her hand on one shoulder, Lucy's on the other.

Eyes wide, Gwendolyn looked at everyone there in the circle. It was not just Dire Wolves, but their mates, too. Some faces were streaked with happy tears, others stoic as they watched Weylin prepare for whatever ritual this was.

"This is a sacred ritual from ancient times. That ink is special, magicked by friends of the Dire Wolves. It's the only ink strong enough to mark their skin," she continued in a whisper-like voice.

"Has Weylin talked to you about our origins?" Sheila asked, and Gwen shook her head.

"The Dire Wolves MC has a long history, a long brotherhood. We are all connected to our past, Gwen. To our present. And to our future. Thor can see it. The map of our lives through his bone deep connection to the ancients and our devotion to one another. We are descendants of the original wanderers, and before we came to Blue Valley to settle down, we were nomads."

"He didn't tell me," she said.

"It's different now. In settling down, the Dire Wolves have found their mates. They found *us*. We are their homes, and they are ours," Lucy said, bringing tears to Gwendolyn's eyes.

"But what is this? What is wrong with Thor's eyes? What is he doing to Weylin?" she whispered in awe as Thor's chanting grew louder.

Just then, the big bald man placed his hands on

Weylin's shoulders, and Gwendolyn tensed. Only Sheila's and Lucy's hands steadied her. He slowly turned her mate until he faced her. Still down on his knees, back to Thor, Weylin's emerald eyes flicked to hers, and he gave her a thin-lipped smile.

Thor slapped his hands, commanding everyone's attention as he lifted something that looked like a pen and stuck it in the jar filled with a swirling, glittering substance. Weylin's gaze remained locked on Gwen's, not even flinching when Thor cut into his skin with the pen-stick.

"Thor is what we call touched by the Fates. His talents run deep, just like his Pack bonds."

"I don't know what that means, but he scares me a little," she murmured, eyes wide as the bald Dire Wolf's chanting changed pitch.

"See, he's using a set of ancient bamboo tattoo pens to mark your mate with your story, Gwen. This is all for you," Sheila told her.

Tears ran down Gwen's face, and she sniffed loudly. Her heart was beating a million miles a minute. Oh, this was big. She knew it was. Felt it down to her bones. Even her new furry half was in awe of what was happening.

Peace, happiness, and love pulsed through her, and she gasped, raising her watery eyes to the smiling ones of those men and women surrounding her and her mate. Gwen was still so new at this. She wasn't sure if what she was feeling was coming from her, or Weylin, or everyone gathered inside that special space.

"I don't want him to hurt," she began, gasping as she watched.

"It's tradition. You see, our tattoos tell the story of our Pack and our MC. But our backs we save until we find our fated mates. Those tattoos tell the story of us. Right now, Thor is inscribing the story of you and Weylin on your mate's back. It's an honor. A tribute. A way for him to show his love."

"I love you," she whispered.

Gwen touched her hand to her lips as she watched Weylin, straight and sturdy as an oak, despite the pain she knew he felt with every prick and slice of the bamboo needles as he got tattooed by Thor. Her heart felt so full in that moment, and Gwen finally knew what it meant to be loved.

Oh, she'd promised herself she was going to save her body and her heart for the man she was going to marry, and she did, well, in a roundabout kind of way. But she had no idea in doing so it meant she was going to step into a world of magic and mystery.

Secrets were not her favorite things, but she

understood why Weylin had to keep this one. The truth about Shifters, the supernatural world, Dire Wolves, Pack, magic, and bonds were her secrets to keep now, too. And Gwen realized how precious a gift that truly was. Living with this kind of knowledge would be hard sometimes, but she felt strong here, with her Pack, with her mate.

She would keep their secret, because it was hers now, too. Gwen was loyal right down to her innermost secret heart. The one she'd gifted to Weylin. Just like he'd promised to keep her safe and protected, she vowed to do the same for him. Not just for him, but for all of them.

Gwen's heart squeezed as she finally understood the depths of what he'd done for her in choosing her as his mate. Weylin had taken a poor woman whose last living relative was a shell of himself inside a care facility to a woman who was mated, married, and had friends. She had Pack now. And Pack was family.

"It is done," Thor announced, slumping down on his haunches as he tried to catch his breath.

"I got you, brother," Derrick, her Alpha now, blurred across the room, catching the big, bald Wolf before he keeled over on the spot.

"Is he okay?" Tracey asked, and Phoenix answered with a nod.

"It takes a lot out of him," Weylin grunted, falling forward, and catching himself on his hands.

Gwen raced to him. She wasn't sure where to touch him, didn't know if he was still hurting, but her mate caught her gaze and, thank heavens, she didn't have to wait another second to be in his arms.

"Love you," he growled into her neck, kissing her there, cupping her face, then slamming his lips to hers.

"That's nice ink, bro," Brock announced, standing with his arm around his mate who was smiling and nodding her agreement.

One by one, the Dire Wolves and their mates walked around Weylin and Gwen, commenting on his new ink.

"Well?" he asked. "Don't you want to see it?"

"I do. But I'm a little scared," Gwen whispered.

"Don't be, baby. Thor is good at what he does, and this is our story. Come on, tell me what he saw for us," he whispered, kissing her palms.

Still trembling with emotion, Gwen crawled around to see Weylin's back and sobs wracked her body at the vivid scene Thor had etched into her mate's skin. Weylin froze, asking her if it was okay, and she nodded, unable to form words for a full on minute.

"Baby?" he asked, sounding panicked.

"Oh, Weylin. It's incredible. There's a silhouette of a woman, *me*," she murmured, her voice wobbly. "I am standing beneath an almost full moon, with colors purple, green, and gold swirling around, but the image is like a progression. A woman on two legs, turning, shifting, falling to the floor and then there's my Wolf, and I am running to meet you. You're so bold and beautiful, good mate."

"I am? You think I'm a good mate," he whispered.

"Heck yes, I do. You are," she replied earnestly. "Anyway, your Wolf is welcoming me and, in the distance, there are cubs. Three cubs circling the trees in the back. A floating figure is watching from above with angel wings. And way, way off are more Wolves, and Lions, and a bird. Oh Weylin, it is beautiful!"

He turned around and caught her to his chest, the two of them overcome with feeling. She heard the rest of the Pack shuffling out of the room, joy and happiness pulsing through their Pack bonds, floating in the air. Weylin kissed her then, and everything else just faded away.

He was it for her. She knew it as surely as she

knew the sun rose and set each day. Weylin was meant to be hers, and she was meant for him. The world might not be what she thought. There was so much out there Gwen didn't know. But this right here, this was all she needed to know. This was everything.

"I love you, mate," she whispered, nuzzling him with her lips.

"I love you too, my sassy little Wolf," he growled playfully, nipping her lip between his teeth.

"Hey guys, sorry to interrupt. Um, did you see Derrick?" Lucy asked.

Weylin and Gwen whipped their heads to the side to see Lucy clutching her stomach with one hand, and the sofa with the other. She was sweating and her voice was strained as she held on to the furniture for dear life.

"Lucy? You okay?" Weylin asked and stood, offering his hand to Gwen.

"Oh, I'm fine. But I think it's time, and I would really, really LIKE MY FURRY-ASSED MATE!" she roared the last as the couple raced to her side.

"Ohmygawd! She's in labor," Gwen shouted, holding Lucy's hand while she helped her onto the sofa.

"I'll get Derrick!" Weylin offered, running from the room.

"Tell him to haul ass and find a preacher! I better be married before I give birth, or he is in the doghouse for good!" she grunted.

"Easy, Lucy, just breathe," Gwen said, lips curled up in a grin.

Sheila came running in with a bowl of hot water. Ariella was hooking up speakers and starting Lucy's birthing playlist, which featured a lot of 80s rap, oddly enough. And Tracey was on the phone with the local church, trying to order a preacher.

"Lucy? Kitten! Are you alright? It's too soon," Derrick growled, scrambling into the room and kneeling at his mate's side.

"Derrick, I'm scared," she wailed as another contraction hit.

"You got this, kitten. I know you do," he told her.

The entire Pack gathered around, moving from kitchen to living room to help with the birth in shifts. Even Thor, who should have been unconscious, came downstairs brandishing an online certificate that stated he had the right to marry the Alpha couple.

"Are you sure?" Derrick asked Lucy one more time.

"Hell yeah, Derrick, hurry up," she grunted.

"Get on with it," the Alpha snapped at Thor, who started the ceremony immediately.

Fifteen minutes later, Derrick and his new bride, Lucy Rand, welcomed the first of their cubs into the world. There were three in total, all girls.

"Oh man, three girls? He is going to lose his mind," Sheila snarked, laughing gleefully.

"Lucky man, I say," Phoenix chimed in.

"What about you? Do you think he's lucky?" Gwen asked Weylin.

The lot of them were gathered on the porch, drinking cold beer and soda, looking up at the full moon. They were celebrating the arrival of their Alpha's cubs, and just enjoying living in the moment.

Weylin's smile spread wide across his handsome face, striking Gwen in the heart like lightning. Oh, but the man was special. Handsome as sin, and tender as a rose petal.

"Any male who finds his fated mate is lucky, baby. But three female cubs at once," he paused, and she narrowed her eyes at him. "Hell, Gwen, it's better than hitting the lottery, especially with all these sassy aunties to help raise them up right!"

Gwen joined him in his laughter, and soon everyone else did as well. Weylin took her in his arms and spun her around under the stars, and Gwen giggled and hugged him tight.

Life was scary sometimes. But Gwen finally understood the bad was necessary. It helped you recognize the good. Weylin was a good one. And he was hers.

"Mine," he growled, dropping a hot kiss on her lips.

"Yours. Mate."

T*he end...*

BEWARE... HERE BE DRAGONS!

The Falk Clan Tales began as my stories surrounding four dragon Brothers and how they find their one true mates, but when a long lost brother arrives on the scene, followed by a few more Shifters…what can I say? The more the merrier!

Each Dragon's chest is marked with his rose, the magical link to his heart and his magic. They each have a matching gemstone to go with it.

She's given up on love. But he's just begun.

In The Dragon's Valentine we meet the eldest Falk brother, Callius. He is on a mission to find a Castle and his one true mate, one he can trust with his diamond rose....

His heart is frozen. Can she change his mind about love?

In The Dragon's Christmas Gift our attention shifts to Alexsander, the youngest brother of the four. He has resigned himself to a life alone, until he meets *her*.

Some wounds run deep. Can a Dragon's heart be unbroken?

The Dragon's Heart is the story of Edric Falk who has vowed never to love again, but that changes when he meets his feisty mate, Joselyn Curacao.

She just wants a little fun. He's looking for a lifetime.

We finally meet Nikolai Falk and his sexy Shifter mate in The Dragon's Secret.

She doesn't believe in fairytales, until a Dragon comes knocking on her door.

Meet Castor Falk, the long lost brother of our original four Dragons, and his sassy mate Josette. The Dragon's Treasure is full of adventure and laughs.

Nothing can surprise this six hundred-year-old Dragon, except maybe her.

Devine Graystone meets his match in Sunny Daye, an irrepressible Wolf Shifter with a heart of gold. Read their story in The Dragon's Surprise.

He's a hardcore realist until she dares him to dream.

Nicholas Gravestone doesn't know what to think when he spies Minerva Lykos on the property his Dragon covets. Can this unlikely pair come to a truce? Find out in The Dragon's Dream.

Thanks for reading.

xoxo,

C.D.

*Dragon Mates & Dragon Mates 2 boxed sets are now available in hardcover, paperback, and ebook. *Get a discount when you buy direct!*

HAVE YOU MET THE BARVALE CLAN BEARS?

Looking for a Paranormal Romance series that is loads of growly fun?

Meet the Barvale Clan first in the Bear Claw Tales! A complete shifter romance series about 4 brothers who discover and need to win their fated mates!

Titles are:
Bearly Breathing
Bearly There
Bearly Tamed
Bearly Mated

Followed by two more spin off series, the Barvale Clan Tales, featuring:

Polar Opposites
Polar Outbreak
Polar Compound
Polar Curve

and, of course, the Barvale Holiday Tales, beginning
with A Bear For Christmas
Hers to Bear
Thank You Beary Much
Bearing Gifts
Bearly Friends!

*Look for more of these sexy, heartwarming holiday
inspired tales soon!*

No cliffhangers. Steamy PNR fun.
Get a discount when you buy direct from my store.

Go and read your next happily ever after today!

OTHER TITLES BY C.D. GORRI

<u>Paranormal Romance Books:</u>

<u>Macconwood Pack Novel Series:</u>

Charley's Christmas Wolf: A Macconwood Pack Novel 1

Cat's Howl: A Macconwood Pack Novel 2

Code Wolf: A Macconwood Pack Novel 3

The Witch and The Werewolf: A Macconwood Pack Novel 4

To Claim a Wolf: A Macconwood Pack Novel 5

Conall's Mate: A Macconwood Pack Novel 6

Her Solstice Wolf: A Macconwood Pack Novel 7

Werewolf Fever: A Macconwood Pack Novel 8

Also available in 2 ebook boxed sets:

The Macconwood Pack Volume 1

The Macconwood Pack Volume 2

Look for discreet editor paperback and hardcovers

<u>Macconwood Pack Tales Series:</u>

Wolf Bride: The Story of Ailis and Eoghan A Macconwood Pack Tale 1

Summer Bite: A Macconwood Pack Tale 2

His Winter Mate: A Macconwood Pack Tale 3

Snow Angel: A Macconwood Pack Tale 4

Charley's Baby Surprise: A Macconwood Pack Tale 5

Home for the Howlidays: A Macconwood Pack Tale 6

A Silver Wedding: A Macconwood Pack Tale 7

Mine Furever: A Macconwood Pack Tale 8

A Furry Little Christmas: A Macconwood Pack Tale 9

The Wolf's Winter Wish: A Macconwood Pack Tale 10

Mated to the Werewolf Next Door: A Macconwood Pack Tale 11

Wolf's Scottish Geek: A Macconwood Pack Tale 12

Also available in boxed sets:

The Macconwood Pack Tales Volume 1

Shifters Furever: The Macconwood Pack Tales Volume 2

Shifters Furbidden: The Macconwood Pack Tales Volume 3

<u>The Falk Clan Tales:</u>

The Dragon's Valentine: A Falk Clan Novel 1

The Dragon's Christmas Gift: A Falk Clan Novel 2

The Dragon's Heart: A Falk Clan Novel 3

The Dragon's Secret: A Falk Clan Novel 4

The Dragon's Treasure: A Falk Clan Novel 5

The Dragon's Surprise: A Falk Clan Novel 6

The Dragon's Dream: A Falk Clan Novel 7

Dragon Mates: The Falk Clan Series Boxed Set Books 1-4

Dragon Mates 2: The Falk Clan Series Boxed Set Books 5-7

<u>The Bear Claw Tales:</u>

Bearly Breathing: A Bear Claw Tale 1

Bearly There: A Bear Claw Tale 2

Bearly Tamed: A Bear Claw Tale 3

Bearly Mated: A Bear Claw Tale 4

Also available in a boxed set:

The Complete Bear Claw Tales (Books 1-4)

<u>The Barvale Clan Tales:</u>

Polar Opposites: The Barvale Clan Tales 1

Polar Outbreak: The Barvale Clan Tales 2

Polar Compound: A Barvale Clan Tale 3

Polar Curve: A Barvale Clan Tale 4

Also available in a boxed set:

The Barvale Clan Tales (Books 1-4)

<u>Barvale Holiday Tales:</u>

A Bear For Christmas

Hers To Bear

Thank You Beary Much

Bearing Gifts

Bearly Friends

Also available in a boxed set:

The Barvale Holiday Tales (Books 1-3)

<u>Purely Paranormal Romance Books:</u>

Marked by the Devil: Purely Paranormal Romance Books

Mated to the Dragon King: Purely Paranormal Romance Books

Claimed by the Demon: Purely Paranormal Romance Books

Christmas with a Devil, a Dragon King, & a Demon: Purely Paranormal Romance Books

Vampire Lover: Purely Paranormal Romance Books

Grizzly Lover: Purely Paranormal Romance Books

Christmas With Her Chupacabra: Purely Paranormal Romance Books

Kickin' Sass

Love That Sass

<u>Wyvern Protection Unit:</u>

Gift Wrapped Protector: WPU 1

Tempted By Her Protector: WPU 2

Alien Protector: WPU 3

Unexpected Protector: WPU4

<u>Jersey Sure Shifters/EveL Worlds:</u>

Chinchilla and the Devil: A FUCN'A Book

Sammi and the Jersey Bull: A FUCN'A Book

Mouse and the Ball: A FUCN'A Book

Chicken and the Paparazzi: A FUCN'A Book

Jersey Sure Shifters Books 1-3 anthology

<u>The Guardians of Chaos:</u>

Wolf Shield: Guardians of Chaos Book1

Dragon Shield: Guardians of Chaos Book 2

Stallion Shield: Guardians of Chaos Book 3

Panther Shield: Guardians of Chaos 4

Witch Shield: Guardians of Chaos 5

Vampire Shield: Guardians of Chaos 6

Guardians of Chaos Volume 1 Books 1-3

Guardians of Chaos Volume 2 Books 4-6

<u>Twice Mated Tales</u>

Doubly Claimed

Doubly Bound

Doubly Tied

Twice Mated Tales Anthology

<u>Hearts of Stone Series</u>

Shifter Mountain: Hearts of Stone 1

Shifter City: Hearts of Stone 2

Shifter Village: Hearts of Stone 3

Hearts of Stone Books 1-3 Anthology

<u>Accidentally Undead Series</u>

<u>Moongate Island Tales</u>

Moongate Island Mate

Moongate Island Christmas Claim

<u>Mated in Hope Falls</u>

<u>Speed Dating with the Denizens of the Underworld</u>

Ash: Speed Dating with the Denizens of Underworld

Arachne: Speed Dating with the Denizens of Underworld

Asterion: Speed Dating with the Denizens of Underworld

<u>Hungry Fur Love</u>

Hungry Like Her Wolf: Magic and Mayhem Universe

Hungry For Her Bear: Magic and Mayhem Universe

Hungry As Her Python: Magic and Mayhem Universe

<u>Island Stripe Pride</u>

The Tiger King's Christmas Bride

Claiming His Virgin Mate

Tiger Claimed

Tiger Denied

Tiger Rejected

*Tiger Tales Anthology Books 1-3

<u>NYC Shifter Tales</u>

Cuff Linked

Sealed Fate

Virtue Saved

<u>A Howlin' Good Fairytale Retelling</u>

Sweet As Candy

Standalones:

The Enforcer

Blood Song: A Sanguinem Council Book

Spring Fling (co-written with P. Mattern)

Witch Shifter Clan

The Hybrid Assassin

###

Coming Soon:

Purrfectly F*cked

If The Shoe Fits: A Howlin' Good Fairytale Retelling

Thrilled By Her Protector: WPU 5

Blood Witch: Witches of Westwood Academy

Spirit Witch: Witches of Westwood Academy

Fire Wolf: Witch Shifter Clan 1

Snow Fox: Witch Shifter Clan 2

River Dragon: Witch Shifter Clan 3

His Carrot Her Muffin (featured in the Eat Your Heart Out Holiday Anthology)

###

Young Adult/Urban Fantasy Books

The Grazi Kelly Novel Series

Wolf Moon: A Grazi Kelly Novel Book 1

Hunter Moon: A Grazi Kelly Novel Book 2

Rebel Moon: A Grazi Kelly Novel Book 3

Winter Moon: A Grazi Kelly Novel Book 4

Chasing The Moon: A Grazi Kelly Short 5

Blood Moon: A Grazi Kelly Novel 6

*Get all 6 books NOW AVAILABLE IN A BOXED SET:

The Complete Grazi Kelly Novel Series

The Angela Tanner Files

Casting Magic: The Angela Tanner Files 1

Keeping Magic: The Angela Tanner Files 2

*The Angela Tanner Files Paperback 2 Book omnibus

G'Witches Magical Mysteries Series

Co-written with P. Mattern

G'Witches

G'Witches 2: The Harpy Harbinger

G'Witches 3: Summoning Secrets

Witches of Westwood Academy

Co-written with Gina Kincade

Water Witch

Air Witch

Fire Witch

Earth Witch

EXCERPT FROM
SEALED FATE

It was snowing, but that wasn't new. Konstantin huddled beneath the broken concrete and waited for the big men to leave. He'd heard the shouting from all the way down the street when he'd gone to pick up his little sister, Alina, from her ballet lessons.

Though his family was poor, Papa and Mama sacrificed much so she could learn to dance. Konstantin was proud of his sister's already budding talent at just six years old. She'd been a surprise to the older couple whose son was already a teenager, but they all doted on her.

Konstantin was almost old enough to work the docks with his father, but Mama insisted he finish school. At nearly seven feet tall and still growing, it was proving difficult to remain unnoticed by the local bratva. That was something his mother feared more than anything.

"Be a good boy, Konstantin. Stay away from the gangs, and criminals," she'd told often him.

After all, it was his dealings with the local crime bosses that had left his Papa with a permanent limp and physical disabilities from the multiple toes and fingers that were missing from his feet and hands. Shifters could recover from many wounds and injuries, but not amputations. That was something even their enhanced healing abilities could not overcome.

The screams got louder, and Konstantin picked up Alina who'd just started to cry. The sounds were coming from the building where his family rented an apartment from Ivanovich. The head of the local bratva had many slums on the city where he took advantage of the many poor Shifter families.

His inner beast scratched and roared, but he was no match for the many members of the bratva waiting for their boss outside. Instead of facing them and risking Alina's life, he covered her mouth with his hands and hid them both in the cellar of the neighboring building.

The old man was yelling about missing rents and

late payments. He was going to use Konstantin's father as an example, or worse, take it out on his mother. That was something, he could not allow.

"Alina, will you stay here? Hidden for me, yes?" he asked his baby sister.

Blue eyes clear as the sky looked up at him, swimming with tears. She nodded her head, already older than her six years and he nodded, cursing roughly under his breath. He prayed he was not too late.

By the time he reached the apartment the men were gone, and his mother was wailing over the prone body of his father. Papa was gone. Killed by the bastards who ruled over all of them.

"Konstantin!" she cried, standing up and going to him, still covered in her mate's blood. "You must run. Go to your Uncle. Je will put you on a ship---"

"What about you? Alina?"

"Where is she?"

"In the basement next door. Let me get her," he said, frantic with worry.

"Yes, get her. I will pack."

When he once again returned to the apartment, he found the neighbors gathered. They shook their heads and turned their backs on him and his family, shunning them even as his father's body grew cold on their kitchen floor. Anger surged, but his mother was there, stopping it before he could blow like a steam engine.

"Come. Now. There is no time," she said, handing him a suitcase and taking the whimpering child from his arms.

They ran through the street, ducking in alleys, and moving faster then the humans around them. Tiger Shifters had night vision and traversing through the ice slicked alleys was quick work for them. They reached his Uncle's house in no time at all.

"You've come," Uncle Petyr said, grabbing his sister in a quick hug.

The man took his niece and handed her off to his wife who cuddled the child close. All the adults were trying not to cry, but Konstantin could feel their grief. Shared it with them.

"Can you get him out of here?" Mama begged.

"Only the boy. I am sorry," Uncle Petyr said.

"It is good. he will make a good life and we will come later," she said, nodding. "Okay Konstantin? Yes?"

"I want to stay with you," he said, a boy's dream.

"No, I won't let them have you too," Mama cred, holding him tight to her breast. "I love you son, but I need you to live. Here, there is only death waiting for you. Now go. Be strong. Be the man I know you can be. We will be together one day."

"We go now," Uncle Petyr said, grabbing the suitcase and taking Konstantin's hand.

"Mama? Mama!"

"Come now, boy. Be quiet or you will bring those monsters here."

That fact shut him up faster than if his Uncle had slapped him. Konstantin looked one last time at his mother and sister, who'd returned to her side. He waved and nodded, biting back his own tears, then he left his Uncle's apartment. And Russia.

And he never looked back.

Grab the rest of the story here: https://www. cdgorri.com/books/sealed-fate

About the Author

C.D. Gorri is a USA Today Bestselling author of steamy paranormal romance and urban fantasy. She is the creator of the Grazi Kelly Universe.

Join her mailing list here: https://www.cdgorri.com/newsletter

An avid reader with a profound love for books and literature, when she is not writing or taking care of her family, she can usually be found with a book or tablet in hand. C.D. lives in her home state of New Jersey where many of her characters or stories are based. Her tales are fast paced yet detailed with satisfying conclusions.

If you enjoy powerful heroines and loyal heroes who face relatable problems in supernatural settings, journey into the Grazi Kelly Universe today. You will find sassy, curvy heroines and sexy, love-driven heroes who find their HEAs between the pages. Werewolves, Bears, Dragons, Tigers, Witches, Romani, Lynxes, Foxes, Thunderbirds, Vampires, and many more Shifters and supernatural creatures dwell within her worlds. The most important thing is every mate in this universe is fated, loyal, and true lovers always get their happily ever afters.

Want to know how it all began? Enter the Grazi Kelly Universe with Wolf Moon: A Grazi Kelly Novel or pick up Charley's Christmas Wolf and dive into the Macconwood Pack Novel Series today.

For a complete list of C.D. Gorri's books visit her website here:

https://www.cdgorri.com/complete-book-list/

Thank you and happy reading!

del mare alla stella,
    C.D. Gorri

Follow C.D. Gorri here:
    http://www.cdgorri.com
    https://www.facebook.com/Cdgorribooks

https://www.bookbub.com/authors/c-d-gorri
https://twitter.com/cgor22
https://instagram.com/cdgorri/
https://www.goodreads.com/cdgorri
https://www.tiktok.com/@cdgorriauthor